ALEX CAGE

CLEAN FAST-PACED ACTION THRILLERS

JOIN THE READER'S LIST

Get the latest releases and exclusive giveaways - sign up to the Alex Cage Reader List:

www.AlexCage.com/signup

ALSO BY ALEX CAGE

Orlando Black Series

Carolina Dance

Bayside Boom

Family Famous (Novella)

Bet on Black

Leroy Silver Series

Contracts & Bullets

Aloha & Bullets

Get the latest releases and exclusive giveaways, sign up to the Alex Cage Reader List.

www.AlexCage.com / signup

CAROLINA DANCE

AN ORLANDO BLACK NOVEL

ALEX CAGE

Copyright Page

This book is a work of fiction. The characters, places, and situations were all created from the author's imagination or used in a fictitious manner and are not to be interpreted as real. Any parallels to actual people, places, or situations, living or dead, is completely unintentional.

TEAM

Many people worked to help eliminate mistakes and make this book the best product possible. With that said, any remaining errors belong to me.

Content Editing
Edmund Pickett

Editing and proofreading
Meghan Stoll and Kerrie McLoughlin

Designers and photo
Devette, Rebecacovers, and Polgarus Studio

To the team, this book is dedicated to them for their efforts in helping bring it to life.

CAROLINA DANCE

CHAPTER
ONE

I remember what it was like to express love and to show care toward others. I remember how liberating it felt to put others before myself. Despite how fresh on my mind those great feelings of sharing and caring for others were, though, I couldn't bring myself to reunite with them. I believed for so long that the world was a cold place that taught some chilling lessons, especially to the weak, sensitive man. Maybe that's why I have become cold, cantankerous, and maybe even a little lonely. Maybe this is what the world and life have molded me into. Looking around, I haven't seen many males I would consider real men, role models, or heroes. Even reading the news, I can't find any great examples of men. Particularly men with brown skin like mine; they typically only become negative headlines. They say if you want to see more love in the world, you have to show more love to others. I agree with this concept, but most of the time I'm not able to apply it.

On this day, I did what I do every morning after contemplating those various thoughts. I got up from my bed, laced my fingers together, and pushed my palms up to the ceiling to stretch my body while yawning. I then made my way to the bathroom to wash my face and looked myself in the mirror, asking myself, "Do I really have to go through another day?" After covering my tank top and boxer briefs with my workout clothes, I made my way downstairs to my gym in the basement.

My house was a nice size—two floors and a basement. Very well kept and clean, and very quiet and empty. I flipped on the light switch in the gym. I could see the small dust particles hit the light. It was an early sign that the gym would soon need to be cleaned. The smell of sweat, musk, and hard work filled the air. I glanced around and saw my punching bags, weights, treadmill, Jiu-Jitsu and Wing Chun dummies, and my meditation area where I reluctantly practiced yoga and various internal martial arts. My weapons rack was just as I had left it: filled with swords, staffs, daggers, you name it. I had just about every weapon you could name except guns, but I had gotten enough practice with those back in my Special Forces days. I breathed in the heavy air. "Shall we dance?" I said aloud, and began my stretching and warm-up exercises.

After gulping down a bottle of water, I took a shower. I put on some clothes and made my way downstairs to the kitchen for a cup of coffee. Sometimes I have tea, but today I was craving a cup of coffee for some reason. I looked inside the dark but organized cabinet and found the coffee container. I grabbed it and shook it about. It felt light in my hand and when I took a look inside, it was empty. Not one coffee bean. *Great.* I was really not in the mood to go outside before having my liquid elixir, plus I didn't like dealing with people so early in the morning. I set the coffee container down on the countertop with the rhetorical question, "How does an empty coffee tin spawn all of these emotions?"

I then walked out of the kitchen, through the living room, and to the front door. I grabbed my wallet and keys from the console table next to the door and placed them in my pants and coat pockets. I picked up my cell phone which was charging on the console table and unlocked it to check for any missed calls or messages, which I rarely had. "Well, what do you know? No missed messages." I then unplugged it and started to put it in my coat pocket. *Well, I don't have many people contacting me, and I don't think I would like it if I did...* I sarcastically thought to myself. I laid the phone back on the console table and walked out the door.

Outside, darkness covered the clear sky and morning dew coated the grass. The smell of the air was refreshing. I really liked the early mornings. It was quiet and peaceful with hardly any people outside. There was not another single individual I could see from my driveway. It was great. The solitude has to be the reason I like the early mornings so much. My car was parked in the garage, but since the coffee shop was just a few blocks from my house I figured I'd walk there. Just as I was about to turn onto the sidewalk I heard a noise. It was comparable to what you would hear from someone when they're jogging—a light pant. I looked towards the sound. Across the street, I saw a young girl on the sidewalk running in the opposite direction which I was heading. She was wearing dark loose clothing which looked like pajamas and she steadily looked back over her shoulder as if someone was pursuing her. I looked up the sidewalk and didn't see anyone. Not a person, animal, car... not squat. It was hard to make out whether the girl was black or white. She actually appeared to be a mix between the two. She never even glanced in my direction as she continued to make her way up the sidewalk. I just watched as she passed by.

Hmm, she can't be more than twelve or thirteen years old, and it's a bit too early in the morning for her to be heading to school... I shrugged and continued walking. After all, it wasn't my problem. The little brat didn't belong to me.

I made it to the coffee shop, a medium-sized building on the corner. Centered above the front door was a large sign that read *Don's Coffee*. I've never met the owner but I may have seen him once. There was a time, maybe a couple months back, when a gentleman pulled up in a nice limo—a limo like the ones celebrities pull up in for their red carpet moment. The gentleman was Hispanic, dressed in a nice and what appeared to be expensive dark blue suit. Between the suit, the shiny gold watch, the fancy sunglasses, and the dark oak-colored shoes, I'd say he was wearing about five thousand dollars. I remember this gentleman entered the coffee shop in a hurry, headed to the back, returned with a pouch and stack of papers, and exited the coffee shop just as fast as he had come in. I assumed he was the owner because I heard one of the coffee shop employees say, "Bye, Don." I remember that the experience made me wonder how a coffee shop owner could afford all that, especially considering that Don's Coffee had only one establishment; but I didn't know his business and didn't care to learn, so I just ignored the incident. The coffee and food were good, and that's all I cared about.

I walked toward the door of the coffee shop. Just before I entered, I took a peek through the foggy glass and noticed there were a number of people inside. *Why are so many people up this early?* I grumbled to myself. As I stepped into the coffee shop, the aroma of coffee and pastries hit my senses. There were three baristas working: one was on the register, the other two were fashioning the drinks. The barista closest to the door noticed me.

"Good morning, sir," he greeted.

I just nodded in recognition and made my way to the end of the line. There were about seven people sitting around with their drinks and food, having conversations, and all had their cell phones out and were checking them every fifteen seconds or so. It always makes me wonder how two people can truly have a face-to-face conversation while constantly staring at their screens... I quickly evicted the thought from my mind.

In the line there were three people before me. The first two appeared to be a Middle Eastern couple who were ordering together, then there was a white guy in front of me with a nice-looking but cheap suit; two ladies walked in behind me. So altogether there were six of us. Everyone in line, with the exception of me, had their cell phones in hand too, not allowing half a minute to elapse before kissing the screens. The guy in front of me kept brushing the front of his suit off like every ten seconds. *There's nothing on your suit, dude. I don't even see any dust particles floating around.* I mean, this guy kept looking down at his phone then up and around the coffee shop over and over again, as if he were on a stage and all eyes were on him. Then he would look down at his suit and brush it off just before burying his head back in his phone. I just shook my head.

The couple at the front of the line completed their order, and the suit guy moved up to the register. The two ladies behind me looked to be in their mid- to late twenties. One was black and the other was white. Both were nicely dressed and fairly attractive. I would've probably been interested in them if they weren't so loud and vain. All I could hear was, "I went to buy this here, and I plan to go here, and you won't believe this, and I saw her here, and him there." The two were typing on and showing each other their phones, just yakking and yapping back and forth. It was like they were competing against each other. I stepped up then slightly out of the line to put some distance between me and them and to give my ears a break from the ringing.

I placed my order. It was a medium black coffee, no cream or sugar. I got my coffee and quickly pressed for the front door of the shop. As I was exiting, I nearly bumped shoulders with a guy who was entering. He was white, black-haired with a fit build. He was wearing a black suit and a black shirt which was unbuttoned at the top. We locked eyes as he entered and I exited. There was something cold but familiar in his eyes. Accompanying him was an Asian man, about the same build and dressed in similar attire. Outside, I paused and gazed back through the misty glass door. I noticed the Asian guy starting to talk to one of the baristas. After a few seconds the barista rushed to the back of the shop. I just sort of grinned and decided to ignore it. As I began to walk, a vehicle across the street that wasn't there when I'd gone in caught my eye. It was a black van with lightly tinted windows. It looked like a surveillance van. It reminded me of the van from that show *The A-Team*. There was a white man in the driver's seat with his eyes fixed on the front entrance of the coffee shop. I thought the whole thing was a bit strange but didn't feel it was my problem, so I blew it off and continued walking home. The roads were still pretty empty, not a single other person walking outside.

I made it to the street where I lived before I heard the light rev of a vehicle coming up behind me. I glanced over my right shoulder, and there was the same black van I saw parked outside of Don's Coffee. The van passed by me slowly. I could see the driver, and in the passenger seat appeared to be the black-haired white guy from the coffee shop, but I wasn't one hundred percent sure. The two were surveying the area as if they had lost something. I didn't seem to catch their eyes or make them curious, so I just watched as the van hitched past me and continued down the street. When they were about twenty yards ahead of me, I heard the engine go into a high rev. The tires screeched and the van darted full speed down the street and made a right turn, nearly jumping the curb. *Whoa... why are those guys in such a hurry?* I thought to myself. Just as the van made the turn I could hear the echo of sirens behind me. I looked over my right shoulder and saw flashing red and blue lights. There were at least six police squad cars. It appeared they were in pursuit of the black van, but they all stopped where I was. Three of the cars formed a half circle around me as I stood still on the sidewalk, and the other three staggered in around the first three. Police officers exited the cars quickly with guns drawn. I dropped the cup of coffee in panic and raised my hands.

"What in the…!" I shouted.

"STOP!"

"FREEZE!"

"HANDS UP!"

"DON'T MOVE!"

"GET DOWN ON THE GROUND!"

CHAPTER
TWO

If I didn't know the drill I probably would've gotten shot because there were so many commands howled my way at once. I had missed my window of opportunity to escape. Actually I probably could've still run, but I didn't see a reason to since I had done nothing wrong. So I just slowly got on my knees and carefully put my hands behind my head. *The price of being a black man while walking outside early in the morning,* I thought. Two officers from the seeming army approached me. One of them kept his firearm trained on me. The other holstered his firearm and then removed his handcuffs from the case on his belt. He cuffed my hands behind my back and then frisked me, taking my wallet and keys and then helping me to my feet. The second officer then holstered his gun and approached.

"This doesn't seem like standard procedure. Can you please tell me what I'm being charged with?" I asked the officers.

Neither responded to me. They just started walking me towards the squad car, one on either side of me. They set me in the back of the car, then closed the door. I glanced out the window and saw an unmarked black car pull up. Out of the driver's side stepped a black man. He was tall, somewhat muscularly developed, and dressed in a dark suit. He had a mean look on his face. Meanwhile, from the passenger side of the car exited a female. She appeared to be white or maybe Asian. She was clothed in a nice, slightly loose-fitting pantsuit. She walked towards the two officers who had escorted me to the squad car. I could tell by the way she walked that she was the one in charge. She and the officers exchanged some words, then I saw the officer hand her my keys and wallet.

"Yeah, this will be a long day," I sighed. I knew this was a big deal. I just didn't know what it was or how I fit into all of it.

The lady nodded to the officers and briefly pointed to the squad car where I was sitting as she began to walk back to the unmarked car. It was clearly a gesture signaling to the officers that they had their marching orders and she would see them later. The two officers came up to the car and got in the front. They buckled up and we pulled off.

"So is there any chance you guys are going to tell me what's going on?" I asked.

Not a word or reaction from either officer.

"Am I under arrest? Because I don't think I was ever read my rights."

The officer in the front passenger seat shook his head and kind of chuckled. The one driving looked at me through the rearview mirror. "You're not arrested," he said.

I looked back at the rearview mirror. "Well, can you tell me why I'm in custody?"

The officer in the front passenger seat turned over his left shoulder towards me. "Sit back and shut up now!" he said.

There was a fierce, rapid rush of energy that shot through me as I looked that officer straight in the eyes. *If I wasn't in these cuffs I would literally knock your head off your body.* The officer slowly turned back to face the front, as if he had read my thoughts through my eyes. I kept my gaze fixed on him, almost in a raging trance, but I snapped out of it as I felt my eyes blink. I knew this wasn't good. I was in custody when I had done nothing wrong and I knew if I didn't get answers soon I could go off the rails.

We turned into the parking lot of the police station and parked in the officers-only yard in the back. The officer sitting on the passenger side leaned in towards the other.

"Hey Pete, are we going to take him to booking?" he whispered.

"No, she told us not to process him yet, remember?" Pete replied.

The one on the passenger side responded with a nod.

Pete stepped out of the car then opened the back door to help me out. The second officer came over to the driver's side with his hand close to his firearm and grabbed my arm as Pete held my other one. We entered the station through a side door and were hit by the station's very distinct stench; it smelled like coffee mixed with over-worn gear that needed to be washed. There was a lady sitting at a desk about three yards from the door we entered. She looked Hispanic, maybe in her mid-fifties. She saw us and stood up from her desk.

"Good morning, Pete and Chris," she said.

"Hey, Maria," the two said in sync.

Maria leaned forward over her desk. "Who do you guys have there?"

Pete and Chris scooted down the hall, ignoring her question. As I was pushed along I looked over both shoulders and commented, "You two are a pair of rude rascals, I see."

Chris didn't respond.

Pete slightly extended the arm he was holding me with forward. "Just keep walking, please," he said.

We arrived outside the door of an interrogation room. The door was open. Inside the room sat a small table with four chairs, two on each side. The table was oriented parallel to the doorway. There was a two-way mirror in the room, positioned on the right wall. Officers Pete and Chris walked me inside the room. Pete removed the keys for the handcuffs from his pocket and began to undo my cuffs. When the right one popped open I balled my fist and twisted my wrists from side to side.

"Thank you. My wrists were becoming uncomfortable," I said.

Pete moved my left hand in front of me. "Not too fast."

He then cuffed my hands in front of me. I looked down at the cold jewelry around my wrists.

This is really starting to get annoying.

Chris pulled one of the chairs out. It was on the side of the table opposite the door. Pete put his hand on my left shoulder and guided me into the chair.

"Have a seat," he said.

I settled in the chair. Pete and Chris both walked back towards the doorway and stopped to whisper to each other. It was hard to make out what they were saying. Pete looked over at me briefly, and after a few more seconds they both nodded. It was a nod of agreement. Chris walked out of the room and Pete followed, looking back at me.

"Hold tight," he said.

I looked at him and sarcastically raised my cuffed hands to about chest height. Pete closed the door behind him.

I sat in the interrogation room alone, thinking. I looked around the room until my gaze fixed on the two-way mirror. I lightly huffed with grim humor and shook my head. I then turned my attention towards the direction of the door and got lost in my thoughts. After some time, Pete re-entered the interrogation room. Just a few steps behind him followed the woman from the unmarked car and the tall, fit guy who had been driving her—her partner, I assumed. Pete walked closer to the wall on my left side to give the other two room as they entered. He gestured in the direction of the partners.

"This is Special Agent Rose Lee and Special Agent Ben Davis. They have some—" He was cut off as Rose stepped forward.

"That'll be all, Daniels, we appreciate you and Williams bringing in the suspect."

I automatically started to put information together in my head. *Pete Daniels and Chris Williams.* Of course, I'd already known their last names, since they were written on their brass nameplates after their first initials. Now I had Agents Lee and Davis. I smiled because I knew they were with some intelligence organization. Rose had just said that I was a suspect. That was news to me, and it didn't make me happy.

Rose glared at me. "We can take it from here, Daniels," she repeated.

Daniels cleared his throat then walked around her. He closed the door behind him.

Rose kept her gaze on me. She pulled out a chair opposite to me and sat in it. She was a very attractive woman with beautiful clear skin and shoulder-length jet black hair. Not to mention her voice. It only made her more attractive: It was very soft and alluring, but I could hear an unequivocal strength resound from it as well.

Davis remained standing with his arms folded.

Rose continued to stare at me. I stared back. She leaned in closer towards me from across the table.

"So let's get to know each other. You heard our names and who we are. Why don't you tell us your name and who you are?" she said.

This wasn't my first rodeo, so I just continued to stare at her. I wanted them to give me more information before I spoke, especially since I was considered a suspect.

Rose leaned back in her chair.

"Hey Davis," she said. "Looks like we have the strong, silent type."

Davis grinned slightly. "That's my favorite type."

Rose smiled and leaned forward again. "I've seen the worst of the worst, so you can cut the tough guy act. All we need is for you to tell us what you know."

I didn't feel they had anything on me so I thought it was time I played along. Plus, I could feel myself starting to get agitated with this whole situation for wasting my time. I smiled, then for a few seconds fiddled with the cuffs I was wearing.

"You seem to be an educated woman, so you should know my name. It's written on my license that Daniels handed to you. In regard to who I am… I figure you already know, since you've been observing me from the other side of this two-way mirror since I got here. Something else I know is I'm tired and I'm being illegally held for something I know nothing about nor care to get involved with. I know you have nothing on me and you're just questioning me to cover all of your bases. I know there's more to you than just a pretty face and you know I'm not the man you're looking for," I said.

Rose was tough as nails. I knew I struck a nerve with her because of her micro expressions, but she had a great poker face. Despite how tough she was, we both knew she had nothing on me.

She smiled then leaned back. "So you think I'm pretty?"

I smiled back. "No. I believe I said I know."

We smiled at each other for a moment.

Rose looked over at Davis. "Please give Mr. Black his keys and wallet. We don't want him to think he's being held here involuntarily."

I looked at her. "See, you do know my name."

Davis walked over, reached in his pocket, and pulled out a small key.

"That doesn't look like my keys," I said.

Davis grunted as he unlocked my handcuffs. After placing the cuffs on the table he reached into his pockets and pulled out my keys and wallet. I reached out my hand to accept my personal items. Instead, he lightly dropped my things on the table and walked back towards the door while I picked them up.

"Smart-mouth punk," he grumbled.

I stood up and walked directly towards the door without saying a word or making any gestures. Just as I reached for the door handle, I heard Rose's voice echo over my back.

"We'll see you around, Mr. Orlando James Black."

I really didn't like it when people used my full name like that, but I didn't mind hearing her say it. With my back still turned to her I smiled and slightly shook my head then walked out of the room. Outside Daniels stood waiting for me.

"Hey, Mr. Black, I can give you a ride back to your place," he said.

I thought about it for a couple seconds. I didn't want to be bothered with anyone else and had no desire to make small talk during the drive.

"Thanks for the offer, Daniels, but I think I can find my way."

He responded with a semi-surprised look on his face. "Your call. I'll at least walk you out."

He directed me toward the same way we came in.

"Officer Pete!" Maria shouted from her desk ahead.

Both Daniels and I stopped, and Maria walked to us quickly.

"Do you know where Officer Chris is?" she asked.

Daniels shook his head. "I haven't seen him since I went into the observation room with Agents Lee and Davis. That was about forty-five minutes or an hour ago."

Maria nodded. "Okay, well we have a tip about those missing girls."

Daniels realized I was listening and raised both his hands up to silence Maria. "Okay, thanks, Maria. Fill me in with the details when I come back."

I thought to myself for a second. *Missing girls? I wonder if this has anything to do with that little brat I saw earlier.* I gathered my thoughts. "Hey, Daniels, you know what?"

Daniels looked over at me.

"I think I'll take you up on that offer for a ride."

Daniels nodded at me then turned his attention back to Maria and whispered with her. I really didn't want to get involved, but I thought it wouldn't hurt to pick Daniels' brain for more information about the whole situation. After a few seconds, Maria started to walk back over to her desk. Daniels led me down the hall.

"The car is out here, Mr. Black," he said.

We headed for the door. "You know you don't have to call me 'mister'?" I replied.

Outside, day had fully broken. It was still early morning and I took a moment to breathe in the fresh air. This was something I have been taught to be mindful of. It's good for the body and mind, especially if you have a temper with the occasional tendency toward rage. We walked over to the same squad car I had been hauled to the station in. I went to the back door of the car.

"Mr. Black... I mean Black, sit up here in the front," Daniels offered.

I shrugged. "Okay."

I walked around to the front passenger door and as I opened it, I noticed Williams about twenty yards away, exiting another parked squad car. He rushed towards the station. There were quite a number of squad cars in the parking lot, so Daniels didn't notice him. I just kept it to myself and jumped in the car. The front felt much more comfortable than the back. Daniels put the car in reverse and streamed out of the parking lot. For the first minute or two of the drive, there was a bout of silence. I really was not good at small talk, and Daniels was focused on driving. It was as if he was trying to get me home quickly so he could get back to work. I guess he had the tip on his mind that Maria had mentioned.

"Hey, Daniels, seems like you're in a bit of a rush," I said.

He looked at me briefly before turning his attention back to the road. "No, I just have some work I need to get back to."

I thought I might as well ask him straight. "Does it have anything to do with the tip Maria was telling you about?"

He glanced at me again, slightly shook his head, and lightly exhaled as if he was amused. "So you overheard her?"

"Maria is not exactly the inconspicuous type."

We both lightly chuckled.

"But to answer your question, Black, yes, I want to follow up on that tip."

"Why not just get your partner Williams to do it?"

"Williams is not my partner. I don't have a partner right now," he said with hesitation in his voice.

I guess that's what I get for assuming, I thought.

I took a look in the side mirror and saw a black van tailing us. It looked exactly like the black van I saw earlier at Don's Coffee. I didn't make any alarm. I just calmly continued my conversation with Daniels.

"If Williams is not your partner why were you two driving in the same squad car?"

"We were both at the station, I got a tip from a source on a case I was working, and we needed some extra bodies, so Williams tagged along. He's only been with the station for about two months or so. I try not to deal with him too much because he has his own stuff going on. I believe he's in the middle of a divorce. His wife cheated or something."

I could still see the van tailing us. I decided to have

Daniels drop me off at the Epic Center. The Epic Center was in uptown and had a lot of foot traffic that time of morning. I wasn't afraid but wanted to be careful. I needed to know whether the van was following me or Daniels.

"Make a right at the next intersection," I said.

"That's not the way to your house."

"I know. I want to go to the Epic Center."

He looked at me and shrugged. "Okay, it's up to you."

Daniels wasn't very easy to read at the time, but I felt he knew I had nothing to do with whatever this mess was, and I figured they had pulled at least part of my file, so he knew that I had served our country. This made me believe he saw me as more of an ally than anything else. So I thought I would just ask him what I had on my mind.

"Daniels," I began, "I also overheard Maria mention missing girls. Is that what this whole thing is about?"

Daniels took the right I asked him to make before he spoke. "Here's the story. I've been working on this case for over two months now. Last month two young ladies went missing. One was eighteen, the other twenty-one. This month two more went missing, one nineteen and the other twenty. All the incidents seem to be related due to the age of the victims and the victims' day-to-day activities. That's it. That's all to the story so far."

I could tell he was trying to stop me from asking him any more questions, but I knew there had to be more. Why were Rose and Agent Davis involved? Why didn't Daniels have a partner? Why would someone who's essentially a patrol officer be working a missing persons case? I took a peek in the passenger side mirror. The black van was still behind us. *And who are these clowns that are following us?*

But none of this involved me. The little girl I saw earlier was younger than the missing girls Daniels described, so why should I be bothered with any of this? I figured I would get Daniels' contact information just in case the guys in the van were after me, which wouldn't bode well for them—but if they were after him, I would let him handle it himself.

"Hey, Daniels, I know you're tired of me asking you questions," I continued.

Daniels kept his eyes on the road.

"But I have one more question."

"And what might that be, Black?"

"Can you give me your contact information just in case something comes up? I mean, you guys took me in custody around where I live, so I'm guessing there is a possibility that something of significance could present itself around there."

Daniels pulled over at the curb. The car was situated so that the passenger side was right in front of the steps that led to the Epic Center. In front of us was a bus station with the light rail train tracks above it. There were many people milling around the area, just as I expected. Daniels reached in his shirt pocket and pulled out his card.

"If anything comes up, you see or hear anything, call me first," he said, handing it to me.

I glanced in the mirror again and caught sight of the van parked about fifteen yards back at a curb perpendicular to us. I put Daniels' card in my pocket. "Well, hopefully I won't have to," I said as I opened the door.

I stepped onto the curb.

Daniels threw his hand up to signal he was leaving.

I gave him a half salute to gesture the same. I walked across the wide sidewalk towards the steps which led up to the Epic Center, keeping my eyes on the black van until I saw it pulling off after Daniels. I felt relieved and a smile began to form on my face; in that moment I believed it was all Daniels' problem.

Out the corner of my eye I caught the van stopping. Two men jumped out and started making their way in my direction. One man was black and the other white, and both were dressed in black suits with dark shirts and ties. The smile on my face faded, and I felt some anger rise inside me.

The van then continued behind Daniels.

I continued walking as if I was unaware of the two men. *This is not a good morning for me, but it's going to be an even worse morning for them.*

Shall we dance?

CHAPTER
THREE

I made my way up the stairs to the Epic Center. There were a good number of people strolling around the area; most of them were going to and from the restaurants and coffee shops. I started to wonder whether it was better or worse with so many others around.

I noticed a shop window that showed a very clear reflection of me. On either side of the shop's entrance stood two arborvitae-type trees. I slowed my stride just a little so that the two men could get a bit closer, then I peeked in the reflection again and noticed that both were carrying guns in shoulder holsters inside their blazers. They appeared to be some type of Beretta M9s. Now I had to assume this was a hit on me, considering the way the men were dressed and the firearms they were carrying.

My mind wanted to try and reason out a peaceful resolution. I thought briefly that it might be some of Rose's people, but I didn't want to take the chance. So I brushed the idea off and continued to assume the men were out to kill me. I had mixed feelings about it. On the one hand I was mad, because I wasn't sure how I was involved in all of this, or what *this* even was. On the other hand, I was excited to see just how good these guys were. I stopped right in between the arborvitaes and waited for the men to make a move. From the corner of my eye I caught a group of people approaching me from the right. They appeared to be shoppers about to make their way through the door I was currently standing in front of. I also saw there were a few people inside about to exit. I glanced in the reflection again and saw one of the men look around, then give a nod to the other man as if to communicate that the coast was clear. The man on the receiving end of the nod slowly approached me from behind. Still acting as though I was window shopping but with my eyes fixed on his reflection, I caught him reaching into his blazer on the side where his gun was holstered. The guy came within ten feet of me, then eight, then six... I waited until he was about five feet from me, then took a couple steps forward and reached for the door as the shoppers inside were leaving. I could see the guy take his hand from inside his blazer. I opened the door and the shoppers came out. I looked in the reflection and saw both guys turn their attention away from me briefly. That was my opening. I vanished behind the arborvitae tree to my right and got lost in the group of people who were approaching from my right. I moved quickly but quietly, and the two guys didn't see me.

I kept my eyes on both of them as I absconded through the crowd of people in the Epic Center. I slipped inside one of the shops so I could see them but they couldn't easily spot me. I looked out the shop window and saw them looking around, clearly perplexed. I had completely disappeared. I sighed, very unimpressed. *Below-average operatives.* They lingered, looking around and exchanging words with one another, until one of them pointed back towards the stairs we had used to come in. The other man nodded and walked in that direction while the one who had pointed began to circle around the Epic Center in search of me. I exited the shop after he passed then quietly and covertly started tailing him. He stopped under a canopy next to a restaurant, where there was a bench.

I looked around briefly to make sure I had at least a five-second window of unobserved action. He didn't sense me until I had made it less than a foot behind him, and by that time it was too late for him. I had already elbowed him with my right elbow to the carotid artery on the right side of his neck and hit him in his suprasternal notch in the front of his neck with the joining valley of my left hand—that's the groove between the thumb and index finger. I didn't hit him hard enough to kill him, but enough to knock him out. I patted him down quickly, took his wallet, and stuffed it in my side coat pocket. I sat him down on the bench, then carefully took his gun and hid it in my coat. I set him upright on the bench the best I could, gave him a salute, and then made my way towards the stairs in pursuit of the other man. I noticed two garbage cans on my way to the stairs. I made sure no one was watching, quickly confirmed the gun's safety was on, and then removed the magazine. I carefully dropped it in the first garbage can I passed and tossed the magazine in the second.

I pushed quickly down the concrete stairway. I decelerated just as I came down to the sidewalk, surveying the area. There was a decent crowd of people hiking the sidewalk, and car traffic on the street was picking up. I glanced to my right and noticed the second man about ten yards off, close to the bus station and swiveling left and right in his hunt for me. I stepped onto the sidewalk positioned so that I could see him in my peripheral vision. I didn't want him to know I was aware of his presence. A few seconds went by before he spotted me—I could tell from the gesture he made. It was the gesture people make when they find a friend they were looking for in a public place. But he made it without drawing too much attention to himself.

I pretended to take in the sights until he was about five yards away from me. I pivoted to my left and began walking in that direction, swiftly dodging oblivious pedestrians. About ten feet ahead on my left there was an entrance to a parking garage. I walked as if I intended to continue up the sidewalk past it, but at the last second quickly diverted into it. I ducked under the gate for the parking ticket machine, and then hopped over the trunks of a couple cars. I waited, crouched behind the second car on the passenger side. The garage was mostly empty and slightly dark: perfect. I peeped over the hood of a car to see the man enter the parking garage, gun drawn. *This guy moves kind of slow.* He made his way straight down the row, checking the cars on both sides. As he approached, I quietly made my way around the front of the car to the driver side, which he had already checked. He continued his hunt down the row. Still crouched, I slowly continued to move around the car toward the trunk on the driver side. I saw the man gingerly making his way straight ahead, checking to the right and left. I gently crept behind him.

He caught sight of me out of the corner of his eye and swung around to his right with both hands on his gun.

I was able to gain control of the gun with my right hand while stabbing my left elbow into his throat. I immediately followed with a left kick to his shin and a second elbow to his temple.

As he was falling, I won complete control of the gun with both hands. I had the gun aimed directly at him as he wormed on the ground, holding his shin in disbelief. I couldn't blame him. It had all happened really fast.

"Okay," I said. "You're going to tell me who you are, who you work for, and why you're following me."

He gazed at me, confused. I could see he was still surprised that I'd been able to get the drop on him.

"Hey hey hey, focus. I asked who are you, who do you work for, and why are you following me?"

The man lowered his head, coughed, and then held his throat as he looked up at me. He cleared his airway. "I followed you because my employer gave me orders to capture and transport you back to base," he responded hoarsely. He gazed down again and hacked in an attempt to clear his throat.

I kicked his foot to get his attention and to remind him I was the one holding the gun. "So who is your employer and what do they want with me?"

He looked at me and I could see the annoyance in his eyes. "I don't know, and I don't know," he replied.

I knew he was lying and I wanted answers to why my morning had turned into a troubled mess. So I thought I would be a little more persuasive. I started to move closer to him. As I took the first step I saw his hand sliding down his shin towards his foot. I knew it had to be an ankle piece and he was masking his efforts to reach for it by rubbing his shin. I figured it wasn't worth the risk and cracked him on the side of his skull with the gun. The impact knocked him out cold.

"Nighty night," I whispered.

I stooped and pulled up his right pants leg to expose his ankle. There I found a holstered Glock 43. I removed the gun and placed it in my back pants pocket. I searched him for a wallet but couldn't find one. I dragged his heavy body to the closest corner in the garage. It was dark enough that no one would easily spot him. I decided to take the exit opposite to the side I had entered the garage. I flipped the Beretta's safety lock on and removed the magazine, just as I had done with the last gun. I then trashed the gun and magazine in the garbage bin near the exit.

None of this is making sense, I thought as I walked towards the bus station. I really didn't know what to think; many questions flooded my mind. I wasn't sure how I was involved in all of it. My mind pieced together some ideas and scenarios quickly, but I wanted to be sure. I felt that I could trust Daniels with some of my thoughts, so I reached into my pants pocket to pull out his card. Then I sighed, remembering I had left my cell phone on the console table at my house. *One of the few times it would be helpful.*

Daniels' card stayed in my pocket as I continued walking. Then I remembered something else. I could feel my eyes widen and a small shot of adrenaline spread through my body. Before I knew it I was jogging, then running and dodging people on the sidewalk. I'd remembered that the black van was tailing Daniels' car. I split through a line of people at the bus station and continued sprinting down the sidewalk. I travelled the route I felt Daniels would've taken back to the station, bending a left at a small government building and flying across the active street, barely missing traffic. I continued dashing over the sidewalk for about twenty yards. To my left was the indoor Epic Arena. I quickly glanced at it as I danced my way through a crowd. I raced through another couple of blocks then arrived at the main street to an urban neighborhood. There were a few shops on the street. Just a little ways up the sidewalk, parked in a side alley the front of the black van was inconspicuously protruding.

I swiftly took cover behind the side wall of the shop on my left. Around the corner and about fifteen yards up on the other side of the street, I spotted Daniels' squad car parked in front of a shop. The shop, funnily enough, was a popular donut shop called The Donut Basement. "Must you play into the stereotype?" I quietly chuckled. I settled where I was for a few moments to think about how I wanted to approach the situation. It would've been hard to slip into the donut shop unnoticed, but if I blended into the crowd maybe I'd be able to pull it off. I took off my coat and carefully replaced the Glock from my back pants pocket in the inside pocket of my coat. I then folded the coat over my right arm.

After waiting for a group of people to cross the street from my side and another group that was coming up the street towards the donut shop on the other side, I joined the first group and then the second, flowing like a leaf with the current of water. I ducked into the donut shop. To my left was Daniels at the register. He had three boxes of donuts in his hand. I walked over to him.

"Hi, Daniels. You may not want to go outside until we talk."

Daniels looked at me with bewilderment, "Black, what... why... what...?" he stuttered.

"Calm down. I'll explain. Let's grab a seat."

We walked close to the back of the shop, towards a booth that had blinds over the windows. I carefully set my coat in the booth seat and sat down with my back to the door. Daniels laid the boxes of donuts on the table and sat down across from me, still wearing that look of bewilderment.

"So Black, wh— what's going on?"

"Someone has been tailing us since we left the station."

I could see a wrinkle of concern appear on Daniels' face. "You knew all this time? Why didn't you say anything earlier?"

I could hear the waitress approaching us from behind. I held up my index finger to Daniels, indicating for him to hold his thought. The waitress stood next to our booth. She appeared to be in her early twenties and had beautiful brown skin with a lovely natural hairdo.

"How are you gentlemen doing? Are you ready to order?" she asked.

Daniels remained fixated on me. "No, thank you, we're good ma'am," he said.

I hadn't eaten all day, so I thought it would be a good time to fill up. "Actually, Mrs., I'll order. I'll have a cup of black coffee, a glass of water, and a sausage, egg, and cheese biscuit. Oh, and can you bring me a steak knife too?" I said.

The waitress smiled then wrote down my order. "Thank you, sir. I'll get this in. And it's Miss," she said. She continued to smile at me as she walked away. Her smile brought a momentary one to my own face.

But then I brought my attention back to Daniels and the problem at hand.

Daniels leaned over the table towards me. "Alright, tell me now, what's going on?"

I opened a slight crack in the blinds and turned my head in the direction of the black van. It was still parked in the same place. "Now, I don't know what this whole thing is all about yet, but I noticed we were being followed after leaving the station. It was a black van, and that same black van is now parked about ten yards down on the other side of the street in an alley."

Daniels cracked open the blinds to confirm my story.

"That's why I wanted you to drop me off at the Epic Center. I wasn't sure who these guys were, and I didn't want them knowing where I live. But I'm beginning to think it won't be too difficult for them to figure that out. To make a long story short, when you dropped me off at the Epic Center, two guys exited the van and followed me upstairs. The van then followed you."

Daniels nodded and continued to listen.

The waitress came back, dropped off my coffee and glass of water, and left.

I continued my story. "I took care of the two guys, then made my way here to you."

Daniels gave me a side look. "What do you mean, you took care of them?"

"I mean I knocked them out. They should be waking up in a little while."

Daniels's gaze fell down to the table and he palmed his forehead. There was silence in the booth for a few moments. I was able to get through most of my coffee.

"Hey, Daniels, we have more to talk about but right now we have some unknown people—well, at least unknown to me—following us. We need to make a move."

Daniels sat up straight in the chair. "Well, I'm the law. Why don't I just go out there and arrest them? I mean, you laid two of them out... how dangerous could they be?"

I sarcastically grinned and looked directly into Daniels' eyes sharply. "That's not a good idea. You could really get hurt."

He saw the seriousness in my eyes then released a faint sigh. "Okay, Black... what do you recommend?"

"I don't want to raise any suspicion, so I recommend you take the boxes of donuts out to the car, and then pretend you forgot something back in the shop. When you come back into the shop, we'll discuss the plan. While you're running out to the car I'll enjoy my breakfast."

The waitress came to the table and placed a plate with my sausage, egg, and cheese biscuit and the steak knife on the table.

"Do you need anything else?" she smiled.

"No, I think I have everything, thanks," I replied.

"Let me know if you need anything else," she added just before walking away.

Daniels stood up from the table, grabbed the boxes of donuts, and directed himself towards the door. He was only gone for a few moments, but I finished half of my biscuit and about half of my glass of water before he returned. I needed to fuel up and was happy the shop served more than donuts. Daniels rushed back into the shop and planted himself in front of me. My mouth was full so I just briefly eyed him and nodded. Daniels was a bit jumpy and out of breath.

"Okay, Black, I think I'll radio in for backup. It shouldn't take long for another unit to get here."

Daniels was the law, so he was trying to take control of the situation, but I've been in some situations where being the law didn't mean squat. I swallowed my food then flushed it down with a few sips of water.

"That may not be the best idea. These guys are dangerous, and they're not exactly amateurs. They'll sense backup coming from a mile away." I thought carefully before continuing my thought. "Plus, I'm not sure that, if you did call, we'd receive the backup we want."

Daniels' forehead wrinkled. "What's that supposed to mean, Black?"

I wiped my mouth with a napkin and leaned towards him across my plate. "That means I'm not sure who to trust right now."

We were both quiet for a few seconds. In those few seconds I felt a peculiar stillness in the shop. The air thinned and a wave of uncertainty blanketed both Daniels and me. We were both struck by the possibility that we could be into something deep. But I don't like speculation; I like information. So I blew off those feelings quickly.

"We just need to play it cool for now, Daniels, but I have a plan that will buy us some time away from the mob squad."

He leaned in and I described my plan and what I needed from him.

Both of us stood up from the booth. I threw money on the table to pay for my meal and a tip. Daniels headed for the door as I put on my coat. He nodded at me just before walking out the door. I nodded back. I then picked up the steak knife from the table and concealed it behind my forearm in my coat sleeve.

A couple minutes went by before I could hear the sirens blazing on Daniels' squad car. I walked to the door of the shop and then onto the sidewalk outside. I looked back towards where the van was parked. I could see Daniels' car roughly five yards behind from the van. I was able to get a good look at the driver—it was the same man I had seen parked outside of Don's Coffee earlier. I didn't see anyone else in the vehicle. The sirens from the squad car were creating a scene; pedestrians and drivers alike were looking toward it. Meanwhile, I was more concerned about it distracting whoever was in the van.

Daniels exited the car while the sirens were still rolling. I observed the attention of the van driver direct towards the squad car.

I ran across the street, behind the shops, and through the back alley. I had to jump a gate to make it to the back of the parked van. I stooped stealthily and with the steak knife punched a hole in the driver's side rear tire and then the passenger's side tire as well. I could faintly hear the air seeping from the tires. It sounded like a light but long passing of gas. One of those quiet but extended farts. I was surprised I could hear anything at all over the sound of the earsplitting sirens. I placed the knife in my coat pocket then with haste I hopped back over the gate and sprinted back through the alley and across the street. The attention of the van driver remained centered on Daniels.

Daniels was looking under the hood of the car with the sirens roaring, just as we had planned. As he glanced around the hood of the car and spotted me back in front of the donut shop, he took a double take, as though he didn't expect me to be there so soon. I nodded, signaling I was done, and he nodded back to signal he understood. He shut the hood of the car then got in. The sirens died instantly, but the attention they had created had a much slower death.

Daniels made a U-turn and drove up to where I stood at the curb. Watching the van driver turning his ignition in response to Daniels' movement, I opened the front passenger door and slid into the squad car. Daniels greeted me with a smile.

"Buckle up, Mr. Black," he joked.

I responded with a slight grin then shook my head and buckled up. Daniels peeled out down the street. I scanned the rearview mirror and saw the black van pull out after us. After a few moments, it slowed down and seconds after that, it completely stopped. Daniels continued accelerating down the street.

CHAPTER
FOUR

"I think we lost them. Did that driver look familiar to you?" I said.

Daniels shook his head. "No, I've never seen him before."

"Did you notice anyone else in the van?"

Once again he shook his head.

I didn't feel I had his full attention, so I decided to throw out a random question. "Are you married, Daniels? You have any kids?"

He turned his eyes from the windshield briefly. "What? No... Why do you ask?"

"Ah, I was just making sure you were here with me. But that's a good thing, at least for the present. It keeps things simple."

Daniels glanced between me and the windshield for a few seconds before moving on. "Let's start with everything you know so far about this, Black."

I cleared my throat. "You know just about everything I know."

He kept his eyes on the road and shrugged. "Remind me."

"Sure," I replied. "And afterward I want to hear more

about your case and the tip you and Maria were talking about."

"Deal. I want to know what's going on here."

That made two of us, though really, I just wanted to go back home and continue my day like none of this had ever happened. I told Daniels about the van and its driver being parked outside of Don's Coffee that morning and how the same van had appeared to be running from the cops before I was brought into custody.

Daniels just nodded.

I told him specifics about the guys at the Epic Center, including that they were carrying Berettas. I didn't think it would be a good idea to tell him about the running girl I saw —one, I didn't trust him enough, and two, I wanted to know more about what he knew first. I had a few hunches but felt it wasn't a good idea to share them with anyone at that point.

Daniels became a bit excited. I could tell he found some parts of my story hard to believe. He turned his head briefly, regarding me intently. He had a huge smile on his face.

"What are you, like an ex-military kung fu ninja?"

I gave him a stoic look. "Yep."

"Wow, I'm in the car with a ninja, commando, and secret agent all in one," he joked.

"You can drop me off at my house," I said. "Just make a right at this next light."

He nodded.

"Okay, Daniels, your turn," I said.

He focused on the road again and adjusted himself in his seat. Gripping the steering wheel with his left hand, he shrugged with his right hand in the air, palm facing up, as if to gesture that he had already told me everything. "It's like I said earlier. I've been working a case for two months…"

I stopped him with another question because I didn't want to waste any of my time. "So how are Agents Lee and Davis involved in this?"

"I guess they were sent here to babysit the police department. The FBI is always in our business. I really wish they weren't involved. I want to finish this case on my own."

"Well, this must be a pretty high-profile case," I said, "with the FBI involvement and all. When did they get involved?"

Daniels kept his eyes on the road then sighed, "About a few weeks ago."

I deduced that this topic brought passion and sorrow to Daniels. His expressions made his face droop, and his breathing was weighed down. I knew it would help him to talk about it, but ultimately I wanted to save my own skin and I needed more details, so I took a chance on a hunch I had.

"So, Daniels, why were you demoted from detective to patrolman?"

Daniels turned his attention on me in surprise. He shook his head and lightly chuckled for a moment. "You know, you're a pretty sharp guy, Black," he said simply.

I agreed with him, but it just didn't make sense that a patrol officer would be working a missing persons case. Plus, why would the FBI have to babysit if the investigation was going well?

As Daniels' eyes rolled between me and the road, I caught a glimpse of the pain hidden in them.

"As I mentioned before, I was working this case for about two months, but what I didn't mention is I had a partner working it with me. His name was Frank Burns, a fine detective, the best I've ever worked with. It all happened before the second pair of girls went missing. Frank got a lead on the case and went to go check it out. He left early that morning and he has been missing ever since."

"What? You mean missing in the same way the girls are missing?"

Daniels nodded. "Yes. No one has heard from him. The

other part to this story is that on the same morning he went missing, two hundred and thirty-four thousand dollars from a drug bust in Evidence went missing as well. You know they don't pay us much in law enforcement, so a lot of people think Frank took the money then up and ran. I know Frank. He's a dedicated cop. He wanted to find the girls and nail whoever was behind their disappearance. None of it makes any sense. The next thing I know, there was some guy with the FBI at the police station, I was back on patrol duty, and there were two more missing girls."

"Some guy with the FBI? You mean Agent Ben Davis?" I asked.

Daniels shook his head. "Uh-uh, some other guy. He was white, I don't remember his name and I only saw him that one time. Lee and Davis came in the next day and have been the only agents I've worked with on this case... well, unofficially worked with on the case. I'm not supposed to be working the case at all."

"Do you know what lead Burns was following up on?"

Daniels gave me a half head shake. "Frank and I were partners, but he didn't like telling anyone anything until he was pretty certain. I know he mentioned he was going to look into something down in Charleston. I asked if he needed backup, but he told me no and to stay in Charlotte just in case any other leads came in."

We were approaching my street.

"So what about that tip Maria was talking about?" I asked.

Daniels smiled, "Maybe next time."

"Oh that's too bad. I was thinking how nice it'd be for us to partner up on this." I didn't actually want to partner up with anyone, though. I just wanted to clear myself and be done with all of it.

"Like I told you, I already have a partner, and if I didn't, I don't think I would want another one. Can't handle another going missing on my watch."

Daniels veered onto my street. I had him park near the sidewalk a little ways from my house. The whole situation was still foggy to me, but I did have some hunches. I thought I'd share something to help Daniels feel better. I unbuckled my seat belt.

"Hey, Daniels, you know the FBI was looking into this case before Burns or the money went missing."

Daniels turned towards me. "How can you be so sure, Black?"

I opened the car door. "Just call it a hunch." I jumped out of the car and onto the sidewalk. I then leaned into the squad car window. "Keep your head down and be careful, Daniels."

"You do the same, Black, and remember you have my card. Call if anything pops up."

I nodded, then stood straight and tapped the roof of the car twice, signaling my goodbye.

Daniels pulled off down the deserted street as I stepped onto the sidewalk. I looked up at the sky in a moment of quiescence. The sun was gleaming gorgeously, accompanied only by a few light clouds in the sky. My face was hit by a gentle crisp breeze. I embraced the opportunity to savor the few moments of peace I was having, especially considering the circumstances. I'd been running around all morning and still I wasn't completely sure why. My street was pretty empty. Most everyone who lived on my street was already at work in a cubicle or punched in on someone's clock. The neighborhood was typically quiet most of the time—that's one reason why I liked it.

When I arrived at my driveway, I thought I'd better survey around the house, just in case I may have had any unexpected guests. I circled around my place, checking the driveway, doors, windows, and lawn for anything out of place. I didn't find a thing. I've had my fair share of unwanted guests, and have been an unwanted guest a few times myself. Due to this experience, I can tell whether someone has been in my house, and I can do it without going inside the house to check. I unlocked my front door and then entered the house. As I expected, everything was just as I had left it.

Being the cautious man I am, I went down to the gym in the basement. Again, everything was just as I left it, but I needed to reassure myself. Behind the meditation area in my gym was a false wall, behind which there was a door with a combination lock, which when opened exposed yet another door with a key lock. I put in the combination to open the first door, then opened the second door before putting my keys back in my pocket. Behind the door was a small closet. This closet contained a large sum of cash, a little gold and silver, a box of tools, a few articles of clothing, some identification and travel documents, and a number of hand-to-hand weapons. Although I knew my way around many different firearms, I didn't like keeping them in the house. Guns always seem to raise eyebrows and suspicion.

The main reason I opened the closet was to take a look at my surveillance system. I had six cameras around the house. Three were outside covering the front of the house, the back of the house, and the driveway. The other three were inside, covering the main living quarters, the gym in the basement, and the garage. I rewound the footage and watched it up until I saw myself circling around the house performing my inspection for unwanted visitors. The footage revealed nothing to suggest anyone had been to my house, never mind in my house. I configured the surveillance system to continue recording, then closed and locked the closet just as it had been —but not before grabbing four knives. These knives were of medium size, good for fighting but also small enough to throw. I grabbed two ankle holsters for the knives. Each could hold two knives apiece. I marched back upstairs to the living room then placed the knives and the ankle holsters on the living room coffee table. I reached into my coat pocket and removed the steak knife I had taken, or rather borrowed, from The Donut Basement and placed it on the coffee table. Before I planted myself in my chair, I withdrew the Glock from my inside coat pocket, charily stationed it on the coffee table, and leaned back in the chair with both my hands laced behind my head.

"Why is it I always find myself in situations like this?" I whispered to myself.

I tilted forward in the chair and put my hands back into my coat pockets. I felt the wallet of the guy from the Epic Center in the side pocket. I snatched the wallet then unfolded it. *What do we have here?*

I fingered through the wallet and found a North Carolina driver's license. The name on it was Jeff Ireland. My eyes studied the address. It was an Asheville address, which I found interesting. I fixed on his picture and confirmed that it was the same guy at the Epic Center. He was white and about five-ten with dirty blond hair. I also noticed the wallet had a few crisp one hundred dollar bills in it. *Hmm... This guy Ireland has to be new to this type of work. Why else would he be running around armed with his identification on him?*

I folded the wallet and placed it back into my pocket. I then picked up the Glock from the coffee table and ejected the magazine. There were six bullets in it and none in the chamber. I replaced the magazine and settled the gun in my inside coat pocket. I put the knives into the ankle holsters, two knives in each, then lifted up the bottoms of my pants legs and wrapped the holsters around my lower legs, making sure my pants legs would conceal the holsters when rolled them down. I stood up from the chair and walked one lap around the coffee table. The holsters felt very comfortable—I could barely tell I was wearing them. I walked over the hardwood floor to the console table, picked up my cell phone, and dropped it in my inside coat pocket. After I double-checked that the front door was locked, I walked across the living room area to the garage door. I opened the door, entered into the garage, flipped on the light switch, and then locked the garage door behind me.

The garage was clean and organized. Various tools and gadgets were hanging on the walls to the left and right of me, and on the opposite end of the garage was the outside door. In the center stood the most marvelous appearance of mechanical perfection you'd want to see. It was my Viper GTS. It was all black: the paint, the rims, and the tinted windows. This darling had six hundred and forty horses under its hood. I had made some slight custom modifications which made it a bit lighter than manufactured with really good gas mileage. The L-word is not a word I use a lot, but if I did use it, it would be in the same sentence as this car. The front of the car was facing the street... I liked to back my car into the garage, just in case I ever had to leave in a hurry for some reason. Being cautious, I walked a circuit around the car, inspecting it. It was clean. I opened the driver's side door and slid into the driver's seat. Shutting the door behind me, I leaned over to open the glove compartment. I then emptied my coat pockets of Ireland's wallet and the Glock into the glove compartment. I reached up to the sun visor, where the garage door opener was clipped, and opened the door. The light from the sun beamed into the garage. It was like watching the sunrise in the morning. I removed the key from my pocket then fired up the car. It roared and then purred down. The purrs were being drowned out by the sound of drums and saxophones from the radio. Jazz-funk with no lyrics is my type of music. I don't care to hear other people talking to the music. I prefer to listen to my own thoughts while the music plays. I put the car in gear and rolled out just clear of the garage door, then pressed the remote to close the door. I eased down the driveway and bent a right onto the street.

I slowly cruised down the street for a couple of minutes. I

went past Don's Coffee, which was pretty packed. *I never noticed how busy it was… Maybe because I don't usually drink coffee this late in the morning.* I drove for about ten minutes, but due to traffic I found myself only about three miles outside of my neighborhood. I decided to ride towards midtown. I knew a tranquil park I could go to. I like going to the park when I have a lot wafting around in my head because the atmosphere feels appropriate for thinking. As I approached the shops and restaurants of midtown, the activity on the streets and sidewalks increased. It was nearing noon and individuals were out getting lunch. Everyone was moving around, much like insects in a colony. They all were nicely dressed, and from the way they carried themselves I could tell they were making every attempt to express their uniqueness. However, ninety-eight percent of them looked to be doing the same things. They took little care to the person right next to them or the number of cars and doors they almost ran in to as they walked along with their noses to their phones. To me, they all looked exactly, completely, totally the same, despite how unique they thought they were or were trying to become. On the road cars were cutting each other off and horns were blaring off every moment. *This is freedom?* I shrugged and promptly directed my thoughts to the mission at hand.

The mission was simple: Reach the park, clear my thoughts, parse through what information I had, and develop a plan. I arrived at the park. The parking lot was nearly empty. I slid out of the car and locked the door. There were multiple fields where people would usually play football, soccer, and even baseball. There was a nice playground area for the kids and a few picnic shelters. I began my stroll into the park. I crossed a small bridge which rose over a narrow canal. There were a few trees and a trail that ran through the woods and down beside a stream which led to a walkway back into midtown. At the center of the park was a small lake where ducks and fish swam. Around the lake circled a walkway that was maybe half a mile in distance. It was populated with a couple walking, a few joggers, and one guy riding a bike. There were trees, large stones, tables, benches, and a bicycle rack scattered around the park. It was serene, quiet, and peaceful. I journeyed a half lap around the walkway before spotting a bench and planting myself on it. I leaned back slightly, stretched my arms out the entire length of the bench, gazed across the lake, and thought.

I gave a lot of thought to what it was I could possibly be missing. I mean, there were missing girls, missing money, and a missing detective, but what was missing for me was the connection between the three. I sat on the bench for some time running different scenarios in my head. I had a few hunches and possibilities. I rehearsed what hand I would play in every situation.

After some time I stood up from the bench and completed my lap around the walkway, which led me back over the small bridge and into the parking lot. I passed back through midtown and drove for a little while, then shot by Don's Coffee and into my neighborhood. I stopped a couple of car lengths beyond my driveway so I could survey the house before parking. Everything seemed normal, so I put my beast of a machine in reverse and revved up the driveway. A silhouette through the windshield caught my attention.

I quickly put the car in park and opened the glove compartment just in case I needed the Glock while my mind continued to interpret the silhouette. It was an unmarked car that pulled up in front of me. I had seen this ride before.

"Great, these guys again," I whispered.

I immediately shut the glove compartment, turned off the engine, and sprang out of the car. I stepped to the front, folded my arms, and lightly leaned against the hood. Out of the driver side of the car climbed Agent Davis and walking from around the passenger side was Rose. Both had sunglasses on. Davis had that same mean look on his face and Rose had a beautiful penetrating smile. Their visit was bittersweet for me. I really didn't want to be bothered with what was going on, but the mere sight of Rose made it easier. Davis approached me and stood to my right. He didn't say anything or make any gestures, just faced towards me and kind of checked out the car. Rose followed a few steps behind Davis and came up on my left. She smiled and I smiled back.

"Good afternoon, Mr. Black, do you have a minute?" she said.

"It depends. Are there any handcuffs involved this time?" I asked.

She grinned and lightly chuckled. "Well, that all depends. Look, Black, we were wondering if you could come to headquarters."

I shrugged. "So I'm a suspect?"

Davis lightly exhaled. "No one is saying that."

Rose took a step closer to me with her hand out, gesturing for me not to worry. She had a distinct coffee aroma coming off her.

"No, we just think you may know more than you think you know."

You don't know the half of it. I know more than I want or care to know, I thought.

I unfolded my arms then palmed the hood of my car. "So what will I be doing at headquarters?"

"We just need to ask you a few questions and maybe have you take a look at a few pictures," Rose answered.

"So you drove way over here to invite me back to headquarters to look at a few pictures and answer a few questions? I feel so special," I said.

"When can you come down?"

"When do you need me there?"

"The sooner the better."

"Okay, how about I follow you guys there now?"

Rose hit me with a flirtatious smile and we stared at one another for a moment. I observed Davis in my peripheral vision looking at the two of us. He shook his head and eyed my car.

"What are we waiting for then? Let's go," Rose said.

"Let's go," I repeated.

"Oh," she added while she reached in her pocket. "Just in case we get separated, here's my card."

She handed me her business card. I put it in my pocket with Daniels' card. Rose started making her way down the driveway to the unmarked car.

"Nice car. Is it a GTS?" Davis asked.

I rubbed the hood. "Yes, it is."

Davis looked at me, nodded, and grinned, "Nice."

He then trailed behind Rose down the driveway. I quickly jumped into the GTS. I unstrapped the knife holsters from around my legs and placed them in the glove compartment.

I fired up the car, rolled down the driveway, and turned left to tail after them. I followed onto the highway. We drove about five miles before exiting the highway onto a road which led into a commercial district. There were office buildings on both sides of the four-lane road. We traveled a mile before making a left turn. Just before turning, I saw a large building of a very renowned telecom company to my right, and on my left I saw a big building of a very well-known software company sitting in the back of the commercial park. We coasted into the commercial park area then bent another left. Davis slowed down at a gate. I read the sign on the building behind the gate: "FBI Headquarters South Charlotte Division." The building was surrounded by a barbed wire fence that stood about twelve feet high. Davis started rolling down his window at the same time a guard came stumbling out of the guardhouse at the gate. The guard was armed with an MP10 rifle and a side piece that appeared to be a Glock 22. He met Davis at the car window. The two exchanged a few words before the guard stepped away from the car and nodded towards Davis, then back towards the guardhouse. The two tall barbed wire sliding gates opened. The guard walked back into the guardhouse. Davis pulled up a few yards past the gate. The guard strolled back out of the guardhouse with a mirror inspector in his hand. He waved me forward, so I pulled forward and stopped. When he signaled me to roll down my window, I did so halfway. He looked around inside my car.

"Hi, sir, I'm going to just take a look around your car, okay?"

I nodded.

He walked a full circle around my car with the inspection mirror.

"Nice car, sir," he said.

I nodded. "Thank you."

"You can pull forward, sir."

I rolled my car window up and pulled into the headquarters parking lot.

CHAPTER
FIVE

I looked into the rearview mirror and saw the two sliding gates closing. Davis rolled up to the front side of the headquarters building and parked, then he sprang from the car and walked back toward me. He motioned for me to crack my window, so I did and he pointed towards another parking area.

"Hey, Black, park over there in the visitors' parking. We'll meet you in the reception area."

Once inside the building, I emptied my pockets and took off my belt to get through the metal detector. On the other side of the detector I replenished my pockets with their original contents and put my belt back on. The difference between the outside and the inside of the building was like the difference between field rations and a prime steak dinner. Like most agency buildings I've been in, the inside was very flamboyant and eye-catching. The first floor had a higher than average ceiling and there were a number of pictures and plaques adorning the walls and support columns. The center of the floor was inlaid with a grand-sized FBI logo—the circular one that has stars orbiting around a shield with a balance at the top. The receptionist desk was positioned closer to the left side of the building, while the right side was more open. On the far right wall was a small café populated by a few workers drinking coffee and eating food. There was also a small Statue of Liberty replica in the center of that area and a number of tables, chairs, and benches. I made it about five feet away from the desk before I caught Rose and Davis strolling my way. I was momentarily paralyzed by Rose's magnetic, dazzling, beautiful brown eyes. Davis's stern, grouchy eyes quickly shook me out of my temporary paralysis.

Rose walked directly over to me and said, "Hi."

"Hi."

Davis stopped over at the desk while Rose cracked a playful smile. "Follow us."

They escorted me over to the elevators and up to the third floor. We stepped out of the elevator and immediately stepped into a neat office area with a number of cubicles in the center. The cubicles were filled with what I assumed to be agents. A few of them glanced up at me briefly then focused back on their work. Encompassing the cubicle area in a square shape were offices with glass doors.

"I'll go get the files," Davis quietly said. "Are we going to do this in the Lincoln Room?"

Rose nodded, and Davis disappeared into the forest of cubicles.

Rose guided me to the door of one of the glass offices which had a sign to its right reading "Lincoln Room." The office had a small oval table in the center, another table holding a coffee machine, and a water dispenser. There were a few pictures of Abraham Lincoln hanging on the side and back walls. Rose walked over the carpet to the glass windows and closed the blinds, concealing the room from the outside office.

Rose pointed towards the table in the room. "There's

coffee and water over there. Make yourself comfortable and have a seat. I'll be back in a few minutes."

I saluted.

She smiled and left the room.

I found a seat in a chair opposite the door and the blinded windows. I sat thinking for a couple minutes. I was thinking about how Rose and Davis appeared pretty square and that they were slowly inching into my trust zone, especially Rose. I was snapped out of my thoughts by the sound of the door opening. Rose entered wearing that beautiful smile of hers and Davis followed, shutting the door behind him. They both had notepads and pens in their hands. Davis was carrying a few files and a folder under his arm. They placed themselves in chairs across from me at the oval table. Davis laid the files and folder on the table.

Rose sighed, "Okay, Black, we never got your story. Walk us through everything you did earlier this morning up until your interaction with the police."

"Interaction," I said. "That's a nice way of putting it. I didn't do much. Not sure what you could ask me now that you couldn't have earlier at the police station."

Rose quietly sighed again then slowly blinked. "Look, Black, we'll level with you. We stopped by Don's Coffee to follow up on a lead before dropping by your house just now. We have reason to believe you may have witnessed something that could help us," she said.

"So I'm an eyewitness now?" I replied.

Davis blew out a sarcastic chuckle, the rapid one-breath kind. "More or less," he said.

Rose cut her eyes towards Davis then back to me, "Yes, at this point you are only a potential eyewitness."

"Okay."

I told them about how I woke up and worked out, and how after my shower I wanted coffee but I was out. I told them about my walk to the coffee shop, what I ordered, and the van that was parked outside of the coffee shop. I told them about how the van high-tailed it down the road just before the police stopped and took me into custody. I told them everything except about the girl I saw. I gave them the abbreviated version. I didn't go into too many details. They were writing notes down the entire time I was talking.

"Can you tell us what the guy in the van looked like?" Rose asked.

"I don't know. He was a little ways off... Your typical white guy, I suppose. He didn't look fit, but he didn't look scrawny either. Just normal build with brown hair," I responded.

Both Rose and Davis looked at each other and nodded. It was a nod that gave me the impression they knew who I was describing.

"Did you see anyone else?" Rose asked.

I thought for a second. The van driver was the only person I could link with certainty fleeing the police. Not to mention I identified him tailing Daniels and me.

"I don't believe so," I answered.

"C'mon, Black," Rose said. "I know you're pretty observant. You didn't notice anything else strange?"

"'Strange,'" I repeated. "I guess it depends on your definition of 'strange.' I mean, everyone in the coffee shop had their faces stuck to their cell phones. That was strange to me. There was a guy in front of me brushing air off of his suit. That too was strange to me. There were also two ladies behind me who didn't really like each other pretending to be friends, which I'd also call strange."

Rose reclined in her chair, briefly closed her eyes, smiled, and then exhaled. "Did you notice anyone else who was with the driver or who could've been with the driver, is what I meant."

"Well, I can't be one hundred percent certain. What is this all about, anyway?"

"Well, can you give us ninety percent?" Davis grumbled.

"I don't like doing that. I've seen where that ten percent of uncertainty can cause a lot of problems."

Davis muttered, "Well, let's try this."

He slid the notebook binder in front of me. He turned the binder so it faced me right side up. He used his huge hand to peel it open.

"See if anyone in these pictures looks familiar to you."

The binder had six pages of pictures only on the front side of the pages so it didn't take long to go through. Each page had four photos.

"Look," I said. "I'm giving you guys a lot of information, so can you tell me what's going on here? What have I gotten myself into?"

"We can't give you specific details, Black," Rose answered.

"How about names? If I see someone in these photos that looks familiar, I want to know their name. I feel I'm putting my neck on the line, so I want to know at least some names."

Davis glanced over at Rose and shrugged his shoulders. Rose met his glance, rolled her eyes, exhaled, and then put her attention on me.

"O— okay, but only names," she said.

I quickly flipped through the binder. I'd already memorized most of the faces. I noticed four familiar faces. I started by pointing at the guy I identified as the van driver.

"That's Brad Evans," Rose said.

I nodded. I saw the second guy at the Epic Center, the one I didn't have a name for. I made a confused look to play it off. "Who's this guy?" I asked.

Davis sighed, "Craig Smith."

Next I tapped my index finger on some person's picture whom I'd never seen.

"Gina Barnes?" they both said with a smile and chuckle, as though they were certain I hadn't seen her.

I circumspectly observed a picture of a man I assumed to

be the owner of Don's Coffee. I jabbed his photo with my index finger.

"This guy looks familiar."

Rose leaned in, arching downward towards the binder. "Donald Felix," she said.

"Oh, I think I may have seen him around the coffee shop, but not this morning. He's the owner, I believe," I said.

Both Rose and Davis responded with a slight nod.

What does he have to do with all of this? I asked myself. Lastly, I pointed at Ireland. I wanted to make sure they were giving me correct names.

"Jeff Ireland," Rose said. "Did you see him there?"

I paused momentarily and pretended to give considerable thought to Ireland's picture. "Nah, I didn't see him there," I said, which was the truth, because I only saw him at the Epic Center. I gently nudged the binder towards Rose and Davis then leaned back in my chair.

"Sorry," I said. "I can't positively place anyone in these pictures there, except maybe this Evans guy. Maybe I could be more help if you guys told me a bit more about what's going on." I was digging.

Davis folded his arms and sunk his weight into the back of his chair. From his body language I knew he wasn't going to tell me anything at that time. Rose shut the binder and whisked it over towards Davis.

"Don't be sorry," she said. "You were more helpful than you think."

"So what's going on... are these guys dangerous?" I continued to dig.

"Don't tell me you're scared, Black," Davis chuckled.

Rose gave me a sorrowful gander. I could tell she was concerned for me and wanted to reassure me that I was safe. I knew I'd be safe either way but it was nice to see her commiseration towards me. "Don't worry, you'll be okay. There's nothing for you to worry about, okay?"

I smiled slightly. "Thank you."

The three of us stood from the table. Rose extended her hand toward me. "Thank you, Mr. Black, for all of your help."

My hand met hers. "My pleasure."

I shook Davis' hand as well.

"Follow us," Rose said. "We'll walk you out."

Davis picked up the files and binder and I followed them out of the Lincoln Room, around the cubicle area, and then towards the elevators. Rose poked the "down" arrow on the console.

Davis held the files and binders in his hand. "Let me go put these back," he said to Rose.

"Okay, I can walk Black out myself. I'll just see you back up here."

Davis nodded and vanished into the midst of the cubicles. Rose and I stood there waiting for the elevator. I could hear it grazing up to our floor. Rose peeked back at me. I saw her and smiled. She smiled back. The elevator stopped on our floor and the doors opened just as Rose started to ask me a question.

"So, Mr. Black... what are your plans for the rest of the day?"

I was still smiling at that moment but felt my smile slowly melt when I saw three men come out of the elevator. I had seen one of them before. He was the same white black-haired man I had seen when I was exiting Don's Coffee—but he was not with the Asian man I saw him with earlier. The two men with him were dressed in nice suits, but I didn't recognize them. They appeared to be in a hurry, passing by and practically ignoring Rose and me. I tried to force my straight face back into a smile before Rose saw my expression. She had looked down briefly when she had posed the question, so I managed to reestablish a smile at the same moment her eyes fixed back on my face.

"I don't know... Do you have anything else exciting and dangerous you want to get me involved with?"

Rose blushed as her eyes wandered around. She was trying to avoid making eye contact with me. "C'mon, our ride is here," she said.

Who's that guy? I was wondering.

CHAPTER
SIX

We were the only two in the elevator. We didn't look at one another; we just faced the doors. There was a silent flirtatious vibe in the atmosphere. I had a playful smile on my face. I wasn't looking at her directly but I could feel the wave of her smile crashing into the side of my face. The elevator finally shrieked to a halt and the doors split apart. Rose stepped out first. We were heading into the main lobby before I stopped.

"Hey, Rose," I said. "Did you notice who exited the elevator before we entered?"

Rose stared at me, her eyes slightly widened. "I did. What? Does he look familiar?"

I felt she knew something but needed me to validate my interest in him. "He must be pretty important, right?" I asked, to avoid answering her question. "He had a couple of guys with him."

"Oh," she responded. "Yes, he's the director for the Office of Private Sectors."

I nodded.

She took a step back towards me and scanned my face. "Black, are you sure he doesn't look familiar?" she asked again.

"I mean, maybe, what's his name?"

Rose released a light sigh. "Alex Bennett."

I shook my head. "I think I just want to go home and enjoy what's left of my day. I know you have to get back to work, so I can see myself out from here."

Rose steadied on me. The look she gave me revealed her concern. I walked past her and towards the main lobby. From behind I could feel her turn towards me.

"Black," she said with care in her voice, "you have my card. If anything comes up or you remember anything, don't hesitate to call, okay?"

I stopped walking and threw my hand up to show that I had heard her. I then continued to the main entrance of the building. During the ride back home, I thought about a lot. I had a feeling that I was in the middle of something big, and the only way out was through it. I was amazed at how, in just a matter of hours, I had gotten almost knee deep into something that could become very dangerous. I figured maybe my new approach should be to aid Daniels and Rose in solving all of this mess. Not for some heroic or chivalrous motive, but for the purpose of getting back to my quiet, secluded life.

I had a few questions to ask Daniels, so at the next red light I prodded in my pocket for his card. It showed both his office and mobile numbers. I took out my phone and jabbed in the digits for his office, then settled both the card and my phone in the passenger seat. Through the hands-free function in my car I heard the phone ring with a rapid ten-pulse tempo. It rang twice more while I drummed my fingers on the steering wheel in anticipation. I pondered which would happen first—the light changing or Daniels answering the phone. The light won. My foot sank into the gas pedal and I sailed across the blacktop. The call went to voicemail. I heard a proud, strong voice say, "This is Detective Daniels. I'm not at my desk but please leave your name, phone number, and, if you have it, your case number, and I'll return your call as soon as I can." I ended the call. I don't like to leave voice messages.

I lifted Daniels' card from the passenger seat again. I maintained awareness of the road while committing his mobile number to memory, then dropped the card back in the seat. Since I was so close to the house, I decided to wait until I got home before trying him on his mobile.

By the time I arrived home, it was late afternoon. I nosed the car a few yards past my driveway and then backed in and parked outside the garage. Before I exited the car I put my phone and Daniels' card back in my pockets. I leaned over to open the glove compartment, removing the Glock and placing it in my coat pocket. I strolled around the outside of the house, checked the inside, and even reviewed my camera footage again. There was nothing alarming at all. I sat in my chair, propped my feet up on the coffee table, and inhaled a long breath before exhaling a breath that was just as long. I removed my cell phone from my pocket and tapped Daniels' mobile number. I placed my feet on the floor and sat up straighter in the chair. The phone rang three times before Daniels answered.

"Hello? Hello," he said, sounding a bit frantic. I could hear the shortness in his breath.

"This is Black," I said. "I need to ask you some questions about a few things."

"What? Did you come across something else?"

"Not really sure, but wanted to ask you—"

Background noise from Daniels' side pushed through the phone. It was hard to make out but it sounded like someone was paging a doctor. "Where are you, at the hospital?"

"I can't really talk right now, Black, let me call you back."

"Sure," I responded, but I was certain he didn't hear me because the busy tone tickled my ear before I could finish uttering that one syllable. I dismissed it. *Whatever*. Maybe I don't have to get involved any further. I had told both Daniels and the FBI just about everything I knew. But then I remembered what Smith had said at the Epic Center, that he had orders to capture me and take me back to base. *I should find out who this employer is and where their base is,* I thought. *In any case, I'm in this.*

I just wasn't sure what *this* was. I removed the Glock from my pocket and placed it on the coffee table. I relaxed back in the chair, in the stillness and hush of my home. The light from the sun penetrated the house, bringing a level of brightness with it. I dozed off and when I opened my eyes again the light was absent, and darkness had overtaken its space. I quickly grabbed the Glock from the coffee table and made a circuit around the house, checking for anything unusual. Everything was okay inside. I remembered that I had left the car parked in the driveway. I glanced out the window next to the front door. I could see the car—no problem, it was good. What wasn't good was the dark, unmarked car I saw parked across the street from my house.

I thought I should maybe go introduce myself. Before I could devise a plan, another unmarked car pulled up behind the first one. Rose hopped out of the driver's side. She walked up to the driver's window of the first car. I could see the face of the driver. He appeared to be Hispanic. I'd never seen him before. Rose and the man had a brief conversation. Rose then walked across the street and up my driveway. I backed away from the window and hid the Glock in the drawer of the console table. I could hear the scuff of her shoes grazing the surface of the concrete just right outside my front door. A few seconds later, the five-thump cadence of her first knock resonated throughout the front of the house. I let her knock again before answering.

"Coming," I said. I opened the door and there she was, just as beautiful as she had been earlier. If I didn't know any better I would've never guessed she worked all day. "Special Agent Lee, what a pleasant surprise," I said.

"Evening, Mr. Black," she said. "May I come in?"

Absolutely! I thought. I stepped back, waved her in, and closed the door. Rose took about five paces into the house. She then turned back towards me with that beautiful smile and a flirtatious eyebrow gesture.

"You keep a really neat home, Black," she said.

"And what's that supposed to mean, Mrs. Lee?" "Actually, if you're going to use my last name it's just Miss Lee. And all I'm saying is it's not what I expected, that's all."

"So, Miss Lee, why don't you share with me what you were expecting? Oh, and where is Davis, by the way?"

Rose tilted her head and poked her lips out in a playful manner. I made my way past her and towards the kitchen. Rose twisted around then followed my steps.

"Davis is currently looking into something for work."

"Oh, I see," I said, directing her towards the kitchen. "Would you like something to drink?"

She fluttered her hand. "Oh no, I can't stay long."

"Okay," I replied. "So what brings you here?"

"I just wanted to let you know that as a precaution we're setting a couple of agents outside your home."

"Whoa, I thought you said I wasn't a suspect."

"You… You're not. It's just a precaution. We'll also have a police squad car patrolling your neighborhood tonight as well."

"Sounds pretty serious," I said. I saw the worry dripping down her face like runny mascara. I knew she had a new development that prompted her visit, and I knew she was concerned about me. I also knew I was the last person she needed to worry about. "But I know everything will be fine. Everything will work out," I said. I could see some of the worry shed from her face.

She nodded. "I have to get back to it, Black. The agents are named Garcia and Hogan. They'll be here until early morning."

I nodded. "Who from the PD will be patrolling?" I asked.

"Oh, whoever is on shift in this area. I can't remember his name."

"Oh, so you checked him out?"

"Of course, I like to know everything."

"Is it that Williams guy?"

"Nope." She carefully studied my face before turning towards the door.

"One more question before you leave," I said. "Have you talked to Daniels in the last few hours?"

She turned toward me and squinted her eyes. "Was I supposed to talk to Daniels, Black?"

"I don't know," I said. "You two are on the same side of the law, and the PD is patrolling, so I figured you two may have communicated sometime recently."

"Black, what is it you know?"

"I'm sure it's less than what you know."

"I told you, I like to know everything, so help me with something, Black. We pulled your file and certain parts are locked. What do you know about that?"

"That's weird. Why are people's files usually locked?"

She laughed, quietly and sarcastically. "Listen, Black, I like you, but if I find out you're not straight with me I'll have to spank that cute backside of yours."

I smiled. "So you noticed."

She smiled back while opening the door. "Have a great night, Mr. Black."

"You too, Mrs. ... Miss Lee."

Rose held her smile and eyed me as she stepped outside and closed the door. I exhaled then dashed to the window to watch her as she slid into her car and raced off. I went outside and backed my car into the garage. I then went to the kitchen and heated up some leftovers to eat. Next I showered and remembered to retrieve the Glock from the console table drawer. I put the pistol in the nightstand drawer next to my bed and went to sleep.

I woke up early the next morning, grabbed my cell phone, and raced to the front window to check whether the unmarked car was still outside. It was. It sat idle on the deserted street in the stillness of the morning darkness. My cell phone was still over ninety percent charged, but I decided to plug it into the charger on the console table anyway. I marched downstairs to my gym to perform my workout and practice. Afterwards, I drank some water, took a shower, and threw on some clothes. For breakfast I settled on fruit and toast. After eating, I grabbed my keys and wallet off of the nightstand next to my bed and placed them in my pockets. Rose's and Daniels' cards were sitting there as well. I had already memorized Daniels' numbers and decided to do the same for Rose's numbers before putting both cards into the nightstand drawer. I removed the Glock and placed it inside my coat pocket.

My next stop was the garage, but I unplugged and snatched my cell phone off the console table first. In the garage I hid the Glock in the glove compartment of my car, where I had hidden the knife holsters. After I strapped the holsters around my legs, I climbed into the car, opened the garage door, and fired up the car. As I pulled out onto the driveway, I jabbed the remote and watched the sunlight reflect off the early morning dew as the garage door fastened shut behind me. I saw agents Garcia and Hogan reclined in the unmarked car. The windshield of their car was covered with spots of dew, but I could see them and they could see me. I gave them a nod then swung a right and jetted down the street. I flew past Don's Coffee, which had a line outside the door.

I cruised in the direction of the police station. I hadn't received a call back from Daniels. I figured he was busy, so I thought I would just surprise him. Plus, if he wasn't at the station I was sure I could get someone to tell me where he was. I knew he had some new information, and I wanted to know what it was. I whipped into the station parking lot and found a spot near the front entrance. I hopped out of the car and strolled right inside.

Seated behind the semi-circular reception desk was Maria. She had her eyes locked on me and smiled as I approached.

"How may I help you, Mr. Black? ...It is Mr. Black, right?"

I leaned my elbow on her desk, smiled, and nodded. "That's right, Mrs. Maria."

"Oh, it's Miss," she replied.

"I've been hearing that a lot lately from beautiful women, I'm sorry—*Miss* Maria."

"I bet you have," she grinned. "No need to be sorry, Señor Black. It's a long story. I used to be a Mrs., but not anymore. I don't have much luck with men."

"Well, I find that extremely hard to believe," I whispered.

"Oh stop it," she giggled.

"So have you seen Daniels around here today?"

"No, I haven't seen him yet but when he comes I can tell him you stopped by."

I heard the door open.

"Speak of the devil," Maria said.

I turned towards the door and saw Daniels, out of uniform and with fatigue hued on his face. He shuffled over to Maria and me.

"Good morning, Miss Maria," he muttered.

"Hola, Officer Daniels," Maria replied.

"Black, whatcha doing here?"

"We need to talk," I said.

"Okay, just follow me. Maria, Black is going in with me."

"No problem," she said. "Later, Señor Black." She smiled and waved at me.

I waved back then followed Daniels down the hall to a door. Daniels swiped his badge and the door clicked open.

"I think she likes you, Black," he said.

"Who? Mrs. Maria?"

Daniels chuckled. "You mean Miss Maria."

I grinned and waved away his joke. He walked me across the floor and invited me to sit down in the guest chair of his tiny cubicle. He sat behind the desk. His desk had a computer monitor and a laptop with a docking station. There were also the other things you would expect to see on a typical office desk—a keyboard and mouse, pencil and pen holders, folder holders, sticky notes, and pictures.

"So what do you want to talk about, Black?"

"Lots," I replied. "I think it may be a good idea for us to... exchange knowledge on what we know about this situation."

"That may be a good idea, but I got a lot going on at the present."

"I know and that's my point. It may all be related. Did you check out that tip Maria mentioned yesterday?"

"I don't know, Black... I didn't even have a chance to. Something came up," he groaned.

"So what was it that came up?" I inquired.

Daniels stared at me for a moment, then he rolled his head back and exhaled. He was about to speak but Williams popped into the cubicle, eyeing me as though he was surprised to see me.

"Hey, Daniels, the chief wants to see you," he said.

"Oh goody," Daniels exhaled. "Black, I'll be right back. Hang tight."

He then stood from his desk and slid past Williams on his way out of the cubicle. I leaned back in my chair. Williams remained in the doorway, thumbs stuck in his belt with fingers dangling out over the front. Reminded me of a Western movie scene where the cowboy prepares for the first shot in a duel.

Unconcerned, I just sat and watched him.

"So, Mr. Black, is there anything I can help you with?" he asked.

"Nope."

"Okay, I'm just trying to be helpful. I figure since Daniels may be a while I can help you and get you on your way. I know you don't want to waste any more time here since you had to come here yesterday and all."

I remained quiet and continued to glare at him and beyond him.

"Most guys come here wishing they could leave but can't. I would hate for that to happen to you, Mr. Black," he sneered.

Anger began to swell inside of me and blackness shuttered my vision. *This white boy has no idea what I'll do... Stay calm... I don't like him. I know he has something to do with this, and before all this is over I'm going to have fun with him... Snap out of it,* I thought. The blackness faded, and my eyes focused on Williams' face. I could see fear larded onto his face and a bit of worry in his eyes. We were both quiet for a while, which gave me the time to regroup and turn Williams' poor attempt at a threat into something that could actually benefit me.

I smiled. "Daniels was a detective. Were you ever a detective?"

Williams shook his head in the negative. I could smell his aura. He was intimidated. What he saw in my eyes was like a truth serum. He couldn't help but tell me the truth.

"So how long have you been stationed here?" I asked.

"A— around two months now," he reluctantly stuttered.

"Interesting, where were you before here?"

"In Asheville, at Chief Arya's precinct... I got to get back to work," he grumbled.

As he stumped down the aisle I could hear his boots scuff against the floor. I looked at Daniels' desk and noticed a picture of a younger Daniels in uniform. He had a proud look on his face. The uniform was nice and neat and he had a charming smile, the kind that sparkled with innocence and integrity. There was a picture of him with a white gentleman and a black woman. The gentleman had a low haircut and looked pretty tough. *He must be ex-military.* The lady had a very nice figure and a pretty face, and her skin was a beautiful, smooth tone of brown. They were at a bar or something. The three of them were smiling and seemed to be close friends. There was another picture lying face down on Daniels' desk. I reached for it, but Daniels called my name before I could touch it. He was standing at the entrance of the cubicle with aggravation splashing off of his face.

"Black, let's get out of here."

There was something going on with him. I could tell that something had happened in his meeting with the chief. I rose from the chair and followed him back across the floor, and then out the same door we had entered. We continued down the hall to the front entrance. Maria waved and we waved back as we exited the station. Daniels paced about four steps before tilting his head back in annoyance and releasing a heavy sigh.

"I forgot my car is at home, and I don't feel like driving the squad car."

"No worries," I said. "I owe you a ride, remember?"

He nodded. "Okay."

"Remember too, we have some things we should discuss."

"Okay, give me a few minutes to put my squad car in the yard. I'll be back."

Daniels dashed through the parking lot, jumped into the car, and drove it to the back. I waited for him at the front entrance of the station. I slightly nodded in acknowledgment to a couple of officers who walked by me. To stretch my legs and help me think, I strolled along the sidewalk towards the side of the building opposite the officers' parking yard. I found an area at the end of the building where there were a few picnic benches and a couple of vending machines. The area reeked of cigarette smoke. I could hear some talking, so I stopped.

I glanced around the corner and spotted Williams talking to a middle-aged, heavy-set, bald white man. The bald man was puffing on a cigarette. I wasn't close enough to hear what they were saying, but based on the hand gestures and facial expressions they were sharing, they appeared a little spooked about something.

I hiked up the sidewalk back to the front entrance of the station. Daniels came out the front door with a duffel bag.

"Moving out?" I asked.

"Kinda. I was asked to take some time off. Where are you parked?"

I pointed in the direction of my car. "Over here."

Daniels hoisted the duffel bag up on his shoulder. I was parked one row back from the front of the station. When we got to the car, he dropped his bag to knee height, his expression like that of a little boy in a toy store.

"Whoa, nice wheels, Black."

"Thanks... It's a beauty," I responded. I unlocked the door and he threw his duffel bag in the back seat, then we both ducked into the car. Our doors were shut and our seat belts were on. He was inspecting the car in amazement. I flipped the ignition on.

"Daniels," I said. "The chief of police here, is he a bald heavy-set white guy who smokes?"

The smile on Daniels' face slowly dissolved. "Yeah, that's him, Chief Day... Richard Day."

"You two don't seem to get along very well."

"Nope, not at all. Around the time Frank went missing and I got my unceremonious demotion, he told me to stay off the missing girls' case. I asked him what about Frank? He said there were other detectives and FBI agents working on that case."

I nodded. "But of course you didn't let that stop you from working the case."

Daniels grinned. "Not a chance, but I was being careful and made sure I didn't raise any suspicion. But something happened yesterday, Black..."

I was in suspense. "Yeah, what was it?"

"Someone broke into Frank's house early yesterday morning. I didn't hear about it until I got back to the station yesterday after dropping you off."

I shook my head in confusion. "Okay, so someone broke into a missing man's house."

"There's more to it than that," Daniels whimpered. "Frank's wife is in the hospital and his daughter is missing."

"What!"

Daniels nodded.

"So that's where you were last night, at the hospital. We have to get to Frank's house."

"I don't know, Black. It's an active crime scene being worked by the feds."

"Look, Daniels, all of this connects somehow. We need to get to his house. You have a key, right?"

He nodded.

"Okay, tell me how to get there."

CHAPTER
SEVEN

I raced out of the parking lot and onto the main road. The car was filled with an intense invisible cloud of hush. Neither Daniels nor I uttered a word till about halfway through the drive. I decided to ease the intensity and slice through the silence. Also, I needed Daniels to answer a few questions I had. I figured Burns' wife was okay—if not, Daniels would've probably been on the hunt instead of in the car with me. But I decided to ask him about her anyway.

"Daniels, how was Frank's wife doing?"

Daniels was still suspended in the intensity, floating in a void of silence. "Huh? Oh Nicole, she's fine. She had a couple minor bruises and cuts. She also experienced a mild concussion during the break-in."

I softly nodded. "That's good to hear, that she's okay. Is there anyone there with her now?"

"Yes, I have a guy from the station I trust, he's with her."

"Her injuries were minor so she may be released from the hospital soon. Does she have a safe place she can go to?"

"Yes, I already made arrangements for that. She'll be fine. I'm really concerned about Frank's little girl who is out there somewhere, lost and scared. I have to find her, Black."

I aimed all my attention on the road for a few seconds. I caught Daniels looking at me a few times, as if he had questions of his own. I helped him out.

"You know I went down to the FBI headquarters yesterday."

Daniels fixed his attention on me. "Really? What for?"

"Rose and Davis wanted me to look at some pictures."

"Well?"

"I noticed four familiar faces: the van driver, the two guys at the Epic Center, and Felix. Don Felix, the owner of Don's Coffee."

Daniels turned his attention to the windshield, and then bent his head towards the floor. "What do you think it all means?" he asked before looking at me.

I shrugged. "Not sure, but I'm guessing we'll know soon enough."

I had some theories, but if I shared them with Daniels it would only be speculation. I'd rather share facts. Speculation tends to really complicate things.

"There's something else," I said. "You mentioned there was someone who came in from the FBI when Burns went missing."

"Yeah, yeah, I— I don't remember his name. Maybe if I heard it."

"Does Alex Bennett sound familiar?"

"You know what, I think that's it."

"White, dark hair, fit build, kind of pale skin?"

"Yes, that definitely sounds like him. Did you see him at the FBI?"

"Yes, I did."

I looked at Daniels briefly. "I'm certain I also saw him entering Don's Coffee yesterday morning."

Daniels gasped, and then followed with a mild slap to his thigh and said, "The FBI has a leak."

"Not exactly sure how he fits into all of this, but he's a player on the board."

Daniels grinned. It wasn't a grin of happiness or maliciousness but a grin of amazement blended with curiosity. "Did you tell Lee and Davis?"

"Nope, not yet. I think we should keep it quiet for the time being."

Daniels nodded while maintaining his grin. He looked out the passenger window. "I don't believe this," he said, slightly shaking his head.

"Daniels, do you have your gun and badge?"

"Yeah, I have them on me now."

"Good," I said. "Remember these guys are dangerous, so we have to be ready for anything."

He sighed and nodded.

We bumped over some railroad tracks then passed through Charlotte's artistic district, NoDa. We drove about a half mile before Daniels asked me to make a left. *From what I hear about Burns, this doesn't seem like the type of area he would live in...* I thought. I bent the left and drove about another half mile before Daniels directed me to make a right. After I leaned into the right, we rolled into a neighborhood of new but old-style homes. It was a bit of a contrast from the surrounding area but seemed to work. We coasted for about one hundred yards. Daniels propped his body forward, then lengthened his neck towards the windshield.

"Hey, slow down, Black," he said. He nodded his chin towards a house across the street. It was a moderate-sized teal-colored house with vinyl siding all around, with the exception of the steps, porch, and one room with a large window in the front of the house. Those areas were covered with some type of stone siding material. The lawn was nicely kept.

"That's the house over there," Daniels said.

I nodded. "Okay, I'll park here."

We stepped out of the car, walked across the road, and crunched over the gravel driveway. Around the frame of the front door there were strips of yellow caution tape flapping in rhythm with the outside breeze. Daniels reached into his pocket for the key, and as he did the movement raised his lightweight jacket. I saw his badge close to his left hip and his gun in a side holster on his right side. After digging for a few seconds, he removed the keys from his pocket. He quickly thrust the key into the door lock and lightly shouldered the door open. He stepped inside and I trailed behind him, shutting the door behind me. The inside of the house was roomy but wasn't as neat as the outside. It was evident that there had been some type of altercation. The television in the living room was laying screen-down on the floor and the couch was flipped over. Across the hallway in the front of the house the dining room table was pushed up against the wall, and a couple of the dining room chairs were lying on the floor. There was an open connection between the dining room and kitchen. In the kitchen there were dishes scattered over the countertop and floor.

I stood near the front door in the hallway with my hands inside my coat pockets, casing the house. Daniels paraded around the front of the house for a few moments. He marched around the living room before crossing in front of me in the hallway then circling around the dining room. The vertical blinds of the large dining room window swayed from side to side as he passed them.

"I don't know, Black," he said. "I don't see how any of this connects."

I didn't respond. I proceeded down the hallway. The first door down the hallway was on my left and the door was wide open. It was a bathroom. Nothing seemed out of place or caught my attention, so I didn't go in; I simply made my observations from the hallway. The next door was on my right and was closed. With my hands still in my coat pocket I eased the door open with the front welt of my boot. The room yelled at me with loud girly colors. *This must be their daughter's room.* There were the usual suspects you would expect to see in any room: an unmade bed, dresser, closet, and nightstand. There was also a small desk with a laptop. The room had a colony of stuffed animals and toys, which wasn't unusual considering it was a little girl's room. I didn't step into the room but studied it from behind the door frame. I didn't notice anything really unusual about the room itself.

There was a closed door on my left, but I continued to the next room, which was centered at the end of the hall, because the door was open. I carefully stuck my head in and saw that it was the master bedroom. It was similar to the daughter's room in furniture and arrangement, but it was bigger and had a bathroom attached to it. As I pivoted back to the hall, the sparkle from some jewelry on the dresser hit my eyes. I walked back towards the front of the house.

My hands remained in my coat pockets. "Daniels," I shouted down the hall.

Commotion echoed from the other side of the wall and after a few seconds, Daniels looked down the hall from the dining room. "What is it?"

I tilted my head towards the closed door. "Do you know what's in this room here?"

Daniels walked toward me. "Yes, that's Frank's office." He opened the door and went in first and I followed. The office was a bit disheveled.

"I'm sure you've been in here since Burns went missing… did you find anything?" I asked.

"No… Nothing that would tell me where he was or how any of the recent incidents tie into any of this. But I could have easily looked over something, considering I've been under a microscope the last few weeks."

I nodded.

"So what are you thinking, Black?"

I walked over to Burns' office desk. "Well, whoever broke in here yesterday morning wasn't looking for cash or valuables. You've been here many times before, right? Do you notice anything of value missing? There was a flat screen TV in the living room, and there is nice jewelry just sitting on the dresser in the master bedroom."

"No. It really doesn't look like a burglary gone bad. But if they didn't come for cash or valuables what did they come for —information?"

I shook my head and scanned the top of Burns' desk, keeping my hands in my pockets.

"I'm working the angle that this is related to the missing girls. If there was any information to gather, you, the police department, or the FBI probably would've already gathered it before yesterday morning."

Daniels rubbed his chin with his index finger and thumb, thinking about what I had just said. I noticed a brochure on Burns' desk. It was a brochure I'd seen before but never gave much attention to. It was for Don's Coffee. I studied it closely and noticed that it identified three locations. I always assumed that the one in Charlotte was the only location, considering that it was new and all. According to the brochure, there was one in Charlotte, one in Charleston, and one in Asheville. The one in Asheville didn't have an address; it just read "Coming Soon..." underneath the location. I committed the address for the Don's Coffee in Charleston to memory.

Daniels was still wrapped up in his thoughts. "So what did they come here for?"

I turned towards him and quickly glanced at his face before walking back into the hallway. "It may not be *what* but *who* they came here for," I said.

I strolled to the living room with Daniels tailing me.

"What do you mean, *who*?"

"Are there any leads on the whereabouts of Burns' daughter?" I asked before snooping around the living room.

"The department checked with nearby friends, relatives, schools, hospitals," he answered. "No sign of her yet. I even did a little checking of my own after Nicole made me leave her at the hospital last night to join the search. But I came up empty. Even the FBI is still searching."

I scanned the framed photographs in the living room, one of my hunches gradually solidifying. I saw pictures of the same couple who were in the pictures on Daniels' cubicle desk. Excitement began to fill my body. I was close to a breakthrough, and then I saw the last piece that turned my hunch into a fact. My hands came out of my pockets for the first time since I had been in the house. I stared at Daniels' face, then uncurled my index finger and directed it downward towards a picture lying in a busted frame on the floor. In the picture was the same little girl I had seen the morning before.

"Is this their daughter?"

Daniels' gaze followed my finger. "Yes that's Madeline, their daughter."

I turned around and walked towards the hallway. "Okay Daniels, we have to go," I said.

"Wait... What did you find?" Daniels sputtered as he stumbled behind me.

"I'll explain on the way to the hospital."

"Hospital... what?"

Just before I reached the front door I heard the sound of a vehicle's tires grinding against the small gravel stones of the driveway. I held my index finger up to Daniels to request silence. He lifted his head in a half nod, indicating that he also heard the vehicle. We both immediately tiptoed into the dining room area. I pressed my shoulder against the wall next to the large dining room window and peeped through the blinds. I caught a glimpse of a black van—the same black van I had seen throughout yesterday, and the same driver who had been identified as Brad Evans. From the front passenger side of the van stepped out a giant of a man. He was a little taller than Davis and his muscular structure was solid, almost like a stone statue. He was Asian, his face was wide, he had no facial hair, his chin was straight, and his eyes were frigid. He was decked out in a nice black suit and a white shirt with a black tie, and he had a newsboy cap covering his head. Behind him two other men vaulted out from the sliding door of the van. These two appeared short standing next to the giant. Both men were black and wore the exact same attire: Their torsos were covered with white tank tops underneath white snug hoodies while their lower bodies were clothed in white lightweight elastic waistband pants, similar to what you would see karate or taekwondo practitioners wearing. On their feet were white Adidas shoes with black stripes. Both men had stern, tough looks. Their faces had the exact same features, not just facial expressions—they were twins. The three of them together looked like an opening circus act.

"Daniels, we have company: the van driver from yesterday and three others. Hard to tell if they're armed," I said.

The three men conversed for just a split second before the twins vanished around the side of the house, very fast. The giant darted for the front door. I pointed towards the kitchen to the back of the house. "Is the back door this way?" I yelled.

I immediately pushed off the wall and rushed to the back of the house. I saw Daniels' lips forming to answer my question, but the answer was traveling about a second behind me.

"Yes," Daniels answered when I was already at the back door.

I heard the scraping of a key being pulled from the lock, then the knob turned and the door swung open to the outside, opposite to how the front door opened. One of the twins stood there. Upon seeing me, his eyes widened and he threw his shoulders back momentarily. His left hand was on the door knob; his right hand was occupied with keys. He grasped the keys in his right hand to make a fist. I stood at the door, calm and peaceful in anticipation, like I have many times before. The twin's fist jabbed towards my face in a moment. I lifted my guard hands and pivoted until I was perpendicular with the twin's right shoulder. I grabbed his wrist and his elbow then threw him in the direction he was attacking. He loosened his grip on the keys. I grabbed them as my hand slid from his wrist down to his fingertips and stuffed them in my pants pocket. It was all fluid and seamless. While the twin flipped in the air I looked at Daniels, who was frozen. I continued to follow in the direction of the twin as he made his descent towards the dining room floor. I could feel the other twin behind me, pursuing me as I swiftly followed behind his brother, who was still in the air. I rotated with my guard hands up, turning to the twin behind me. There was a heavy thump from the first twin finishing his plunge to the floor, followed by the brazen crash of the front door being bashed open by the giant. Meanwhile, twin number two lobbed at me with a right cross, fast—but I'd seen much faster. I parried his right cross then struck him with a chop to his neck, directly in the area where the transverse cervical nerve rested. I threw my arm over then under his arm, hooking it between my bicep and forearm. I spun to my left then planted my elbow in between his chest and solar plexus. The momentum from his punch, combined with the torsion from me spinning, sent him soaring over my hip through the air and then on top of his brother.

My attention momentarily diverted to the front of the house. The giant took two long, booming strides across the hallway, then he was in the dining room and Daniels was in his path. Daniels was struggling to unholster his gun. I calculated that by the time Daniels was able to unholster it, the giant would already be on him.

My location was just behind the kitchen area towards the

back side of the house. I dashed towards the front. Daniels managed to unholster his gun but stumbled over one of the dining room chairs. His fall was broken by the table cornered up against the side wall. The giant was only an arm's length from him. As I sprinted to the front I delivered a hard stomp to the stomach of the second twin, the force traveling through his stomach, out his back, and into the stomach of his brother, who was wedged underneath him. I could hear both of them gasp out a cough of pain.

I immediately heard something else: the sound of the giant flinging Daniels' gun out of his hand. The gun cracked through the large dining room window. When I reached them, the giant had his hand around Daniels' throat, suspending him in the air. Daniels was kicking, clawing, and fighting. I reacted quickly with a round kick to the giant's stomach. He promptly released his grip on Daniels' neck, bent over, and hugged his stomach, while Daniels' feet hit the floor, his body jerked backwards against the dining room table, and he held his throat, coughing and panting.

"Get out of here!" I yelled at him.

The giant directed his attention towards me. He gritted his teeth and growled under his breath. Daniels raced to the front door as the giant stood up straight facing me.

I knew I had to put forth a little more effort in my next attack. I evaluated the situation. We were outnumbered two to one when I included Evans, who was outside. Daniels had lost his gun and, besides, wasn't exactly built to tango with these types of guys. It would be a matter of seconds before the twins wrestled back to their feet. I sunk back and channeled my energy. The giant began to loom over me. I jumped in the air, my body in a tight ball, and then I pushed out my legs and arms in midair. It was as if I was lying down and stretching out on an invisible bed in the air but violently bursting out with a ton of force. The heels of my right and left feet pounded into the stomach and rib cage on both sides of the giant's core. I saw him stagger back towards the dining room window as my body continued to flip backwards in the air. That split second in the air felt like a couple of minutes. Looking up towards the ceiling, I caught a glimpse of my boots folding behind me, got a view of the back of the house, and beheld the twins laid out over one another, cradling their stomachs in pain. I finally saw the floor and purposefully landed with my right knee and my right fist firmly against it. My head lifted up as I looked to the front of the house. At the open door I could see the dust particles swirling in the light of the sun.

Reeling from the effect of my strike, the giant smashed backwards through the dining room window and onto the outside porch. I leaped through the massive hole he created and thumped down on the porch. I stood over him and briefly watched him rock from side to side, trying to shake off the impact of his fall. My gaze briefly caught Daniels plowing across the gravel of the driveway. He was going for his gun, which lay slightly covered in the gravel. I hopped off the porch and thought triumphantly, *We're winning.*

That thought was short-lived.

Evans stood at the front of the van with his gun in hand. It was the same type of gun both Ireland and Smith were carrying at the Epic Center, a black Beretta M9, but this one had a suppressor. I hustled towards him while lifting my bottom right pants leg and removing one of the knives from my ankle holster. Evans started to raise the pistol. Daniels was crouched over, digging through the gravel to get his gun. My right arm was cocking the knife back over my right shoulder. Evans' feet settled into shooting position. I wasn't sure if he was going to shoot Daniels or just tell him to freeze. Either way, I didn't care; it wasn't a chance I wanted to take. Daniels clasped his gun with both hands over the gravel. Evans leveled his gun, and Daniels was a little over one second away from being in its sights. I looked into the future, and I could see where Evans' hand would be in the next second. My arm catapulted forward, my hand gently released, and the knife cut through the air right into the future.

The knife gashed into his left hand—his guide hand. The shock caused him to drop the gun, and by that time I was already at his side. I twisted my hip and swung my right elbow. My elbow struck him on the left side of his face, connecting between his upper jaw bone and his temple. His head smacked into the hood of the van. I kicked his gun underneath the van. Daniels was up on his feet now.

I nodded towards the car and yelled, "Let's go!"

Daniels nodded in agreement.

We mashed across the gravel driveway and across the road. I arrived at the car first, quickly unlocked the doors, and dived into the car. Daniels ducked in a second after me. I already had the keys in the ignition and the car fired up.

"Okay let's go, let's go!" Daniels panted.

I angled the car left and bolted over the asphalt.

CHAPTER
EIGHT

We flew out of the neighborhood, ran a few lights, and made a number of turns. We were not followed. We were at least two miles away from Burns' home before we started to talk.

"Who were those guys?" Daniels nervously asked .

"I'm not sure who they are."

"How would they know what your car looks like?"

I thought about it for a second and figured that maybe Williams or Day saw my car at the police station earlier. Plus, Bennett works for the FBI, so it wouldn't be too difficult for him to look up my car.

"I can think of a few ways how," I answered.

Daniels glanced over at me. "What did you say you do for a living? Black, you were incredible. I couldn't even keep up with you. Lucky for us you were so fast."

"Which hospital is Burns' wife in?"

"The Carolina Medical Center."

"Okay, that's where we're heading now."

"I'm not sure what's going on here, Black."

"I'm not one hundred percent sure myself, but I know the break-in was not a burglary and I know whoever's behind this is panicking. They came after us in broad daylight. I might have been able to overlook the Epic Center incident yesterday, but today settles it. These guys are running short on time."

Daniels faced the front and stared into space for a few seconds. I kept my hands on the steering wheel, eyes fixed on the road and the rearview mirrors to make sure we were not being followed. Daniels pulled out his cell phone then poked at the screen for a few seconds before holding it to his ear. My attention held steady on the road.

"How's everything there?" Daniels asked into the phone. He listened for a few moments. "Oh, so the doctor is letting her leave?"

I looked at him from the corner of my eye.

He continued to look forward and listen to the muffled voice on the other side of the phone. "Uh-huh, tell her to get ready and make sure she has all of her things. I'll be there in about ten… fifteen minutes," Daniels uttered into the phone. He ended his call and turned his attention towards me.

"Looks like the doctor is gonna let Nicole leave today. I figure I'll take her out of town to some of her relatives until we figure all this out."

"Good idea."

Daniels tilted his head back in the seat until it rested almost parallel to the roof of the car. He surrendered a lengthy bass sigh, the type of sigh you release when you've been through the first wave of enemies, but you know there are even more waves to come, so you take a moment to relax. The imprint from the giant's hand was still prominent around his neck. I could tell he was a bit out of his element. Distress dripped down the side of his face like hot wax off a candle.

"Hey, Daniels."

"Yeah," he said, but kept his head tilted back facing the roof of the car.

"What do you think about having a talk with Rose and Davis about what transpired?"

Daniels faced me as he slowly straightened up in the seat. "I don't know, Black. You did say there was a leak in the FBI."

"Yeah, but I don't believe Rose and Davis have anything to do with it."

"But they're part of the Bureau. Do we really want to take that chance?"

"Well, you're part of the PD and I'm sure the PD has a leak too, but here I am working with you."

Daniels briefly cut his gaze from me and stared at the floor in thought. Then he looked at me again.

"What makes you think there's a leak in the PD?"

With my eyes on the road I considered his question for a couple seconds.

"How does two hundred and thirty-four thousand dollars go missing from the PD without there being a leak?" I asked. "Unless you believe Burns took the money after all."

"I see what you mean," Daniels said.

"I believe Rose and Davis can help fill in the gaps. Plus, a little extra help, especially from someone in the agency, wouldn't be a bad thing right now."

"Maybe you're right, Black."

I looked over at Daniels. He seemed a bit relieved, but I could still see the worry splashed over his face.

"But first things first—let's get to Nicole and make sure she's okay," I said.

I wheeled the car into the parking lot of the hospital. Both Daniels and I jumped out and dashed towards the entrance. We stepped through the sliding glass doors. The lobby was quiet. I noticed an odor, but it wasn't the usual horrible stench hospitals typically reek of. It was a blend of coffee and flowers. It could've just been a sign that I wanted coffee—I tend to smell coffee when I'm craving a cup.

Adhering to a habit of mine, I scanned the floor for my ETWs: exits, threats, and possible weapons. I saw two other exits on the floor, excluding the main doors. There was also an entrance to the stairwell. There weren't many people in the reception area, just a few nurses and one or two people coming in behind us. So no threats. And there were a number of possible weapons that could be used.

"This way, Black," Daniels called to me as he raced towards the elevators.

He pushed the "up" arrow on the elevator's control console.

"What floor is she on?" I asked.

"Four," Daniels replied. "Room four-zero-nine."

I started in the direction of the stairwell. "Okay, I'll meet you up there."

"Wait, Black, where are you going?"

I turned back towards Daniels. "I feel like taking the stairs. I'll see you up there."

He shrugged.

I continued to the stairwell. I wanted to be extra cautious, so I thought it would be a good idea to check the stairwell and get a lay of the land for the fourth floor before exiting onto it from the elevator. Just before I entered the stairwell, I heard the ding of the elevator—the ding it makes moments before the doors pull open. I carefully sprinted up the empty stairwell. I cracked the door leading onto the fourth floor and peeped through the crack for a speedy preliminary survey. I noted no suspicious activity. I turned the doorknob then pulled the handle and the door swung open into the stairwell. I slid down the hallway across the silky cement tile floor, passing a number of rooms, a few nurses, and a doctor on my way to the elevators. One of the rooms I passed was room four-zero-nine. There was a man sitting outside of the room and the door was closed. He had his head bent downward looking into the screen of his cell phone. He looked up at me as I passed with curiosity and vigilance in his eyes. I continued towards the elevators. A few seconds later the elevator dinged and Daniels stepped out.

"Oh you already made it up here," he said. Daniels pointed in the direction from which I came. "This way."

We journeyed back down the hall to room four-zero-nine, and I trailed a few steps behind Daniels. The man in front of the room stood up from the chair and greeted us with a friendly grin.

He and Daniels then shook hands. "Thanks so much for helping out," Daniels said.

"Burns is like family. I'd do anything to help," the man said. "So you must be Black. I saw you walking down the hall but didn't know who you were. Good to meet you," he nodded.

I nodded back. "Same here."

Daniels stepped over to the room door. "Is she in here?" he asked the man.

"Yes, she should be finishing up her packing now."

Daniels knuckled two light knocks upon the door. There was a silence. Daniels then delivered two more knocks.

A soft voice echoed from the other side of the door. "Who's there?"

"It's me, Pete."

"It's unlocked," the voice said.

Daniels gently pushed against the door, propped the door open, and then stepped into the room. I heard a moment of weeping and faint conversation breezing out from the room. Less than thirty seconds later a naturally beautiful black woman strolled out the room. She was the same lady I had seen in the pictures, but the pictures did her no justice. She had brown milky-smooth skin, puffed natural curly hair, and a body that advertised that she was a woman who took care of herself. She had her purse strapped over her shoulders. She looked healthy—she looked like she was going shopping, not leaving the hospital. Without knowing, it would've been hard to imagine she was ever in a hospital. She was a natural black queen. With a smile, she acknowledged the man who was sitting outside of her room. Then she looked towards me. She browsed my face with a blend of confusion, relief, suspicion, and curiosity. She didn't know what to make of me. I smiled to reassure her I was friendly and she forced a smile in return. Daniels stepped out of the room behind her, carrying a tote bag.

"Nicole, this is Mr. Black. Black, this is Nicole Burns," Daniels said.

"Nice to meet you, Mr. Black," she said.

"Likewise, ma'am."

Daniels started talking to the other gentleman and they walked a few steps up the hall towards the elevators. Nicole stared at me. It wasn't an intrusive or malicious stare—nothing negative in it. It was more a stare of wonder. It circumscribed a cloud of awkwardness around us. I understood. She had been through a lot over the last few weeks.

I decided to break the awkwardness with a question. "How are you feeling, Mrs. Burns?"

Nicole sighed then looked down at the floor. "I'm doing well, considering the circumstances. I'm thankful I have some nosy neighbors who work from home all day. If it wasn't for them seeing the front door open and calling 9-1-1, my minor injuries could have been more serious," she said.

"Do you remember anything from the break-in?"

She shook her head. "I can't remember much... it all happened so fast. I remember a couple of guys dressed in black with black masks, similar to what you would see a cat burglar wearing. Outside of that... hearing some commotion... seeing my daughter run out the front door and waking up in the hospital, I don't remember anything else."

I nodded. "Did the neighbor see anything?"

Nicole lifted a genuine smile on her face. "You are direct and straight to it, aren't you? You remind me of the two most important men I have in my life."

I gave her a semi-gawk look. She'd caught me off guard. "Ah... what do you mean?"

She held her smile and batted her eyes once. "You remind me of my father Colonel Derrick Buckler. Hard, serious, and to the point. Always planning and connecting the dots."

I smiled but the name didn't ring any bells for me. "So your father served?"

"He is currently serving, but to answer your question, the neighbor didn't see anything. I believe they mentioned they heard a vehicle pulling off."

"I see, Mrs. Burns. I have one more question. Do you have your house key?"

She tilted her head, looking a bit confused, and said, "Yes, I do, they're right here in my purse."

Nicole slid her keys out of her purse then held them up in front of her face. "See, here they are," she said as she placed the keys back in her purse. "Why did you ask me that, Mr. Black?"

I was just about to ask her a question about her husband but Daniels interrupted us.

"You ready?" Daniels asked Nicole.

I was happy for Daniels' perfectly timed interlude since I didn't know how Nicole would feel about answering a question concerning her husband.

"Sure," Nicole answered.

Nicole, Daniels, and I walked towards the elevators. The man who had been sitting outside the room was already at the elevators fetching a ride downstairs for the four of us. The elevator dinged then the doors bopped open and we got in.

I started towards the stairwell. "I'll see you guys downstairs."

Confusion struck Nicole's face. "You're not coming down with us?"

Daniels gently laid his hand on her back. "He likes to take the stairs," he whispered.

The confusion wiped off Nicole's face and was replaced with calm as the elevator doors thumped closed.

I marched to the stairwell and headed for the lobby. I looked around but didn't notice anything that was cause for alarm. Daniels and the bunch hadn't made it down yet so I walked outside the front door just to survey the outside and of course check on my car. Everything was quiet, everything was in check. I slipped back into the lobby. I was greeted by Nicole and Daniels just steps from the front entrance.

"Where's your friend?" I asked Daniels.

"He went to get the car. He'll be bringing it around to the front."

"Okay, while we wait for him, I'm going to the restroom," I said.

I walked across the lobby past the receptionist desk where the bathrooms were located. The bathroom was surprisingly tight and clean and larger than most. Someone else walked in behind me. He was a young-looking guy, maybe twenty-four or twenty-five. He had nice, slick black hair with a well-groomed full beard, straight teeth, and a fit build. Not the build of a professional soldier or a competitive martial artist, but a build you would receive from visiting the gym a few times a week. I figured he worked at the hospital because he was wearing loosely fitted light green scrubs. As I relieved myself at one of the urinals, he stood two urinals down from me. I flushed then scuffed across the floor to the sinks. I heard the guy flush his urinal. I reached to turn on the water to wash my hands and caught the guy's reflection in the mirror. He was about to leave the restroom without washing his hands. I was taken aback. This little punk didn't even have the decency to wash his hands so no one would catch his tiny baby crabs... If we were out on the battlefield, where such luxuries as water and soap didn't exist, that would be one thing. But these luxuries are too often taken for granted in the civilian world. I became uneasy.

"You're going to walk out without washing your hands," I called to the guy.

The guy turned around in shock, but then a look of offense splashed on his face. He glared at me as if I had no right to say anything to him, as if his bad hygiene was okay and had nothing to do with those around him. With a grim face I dared him to say something. I dared him to make a move. There was no way I was going to let that little soft privileged boy get away with it. The seriousness on his face transformed into a visage of apology. I remained stern.

"O— oh yeah," he said. "Sometimes I forget."

My gazed stayed on him as he walked over to the sink, washed and dried his hands, and then walked out of the bathroom. I watched him the whole time and thought to myself, *You didn't forget, you're just inconsiderate, nasty, and never learned your stuff stinks.* When he left I was in the restroom alone, and I washed and dried my hands. I looked into the mirror and exhaled. I was still on the fence about being involved with the mess I was in. I knew the person behind this saw me as a threat, so I had to get through it. I just didn't have the motivation. I mean, I kind of cared about the missing girls, Burns, and his daughter, but I didn't really know them. So how was any of it my problem?

I reached into my pocket and pulled out the keys I had taken from one of the twins at the Burns' house. It was a key chain. There was a key for a Chevy vehicle, a house key, and a small key. The small key looked to be for some type of small safe or maybe even a P.O. box. *I'm certain these keys belong to you, Burns, but I'm not exactly sure where you are.*

CHAPTER
NINE

I made my way back into the hospital lobby. I saw Daniels and I saw Nicole, but they weren't alone. Standing with them were Agent Rose and Agent Davis. As always, it was a bitter-sweet feeling I experienced when I saw those two. On one hand, I loved to see Rose, but on the other hand her appearance was a reminder of my involvement in this whole chaos.

"Great," I whispered under my breath.

As I made my way closer to the group, I could hear the echoes of light argument. Rose and Daniels were having a round of words with one another.

I heard Daniels utter, "You don't know him or his family."

Rose fired off, "That was an active FBI crime scene. You shouldn't be on this case anyway."

Davis was in between them, playing the peacemaker. I looked at Nicole. Distress was oozing down her face. I still had a bit of anger from my restroom visit, so I used that adrenaline to get between Rose and Daniels.

"Listen, you two," I said. "You're on the same team. Both of you need to calm down. I believe you both are dedicated to the law, so we have to work together. Let's remember the real victims here: Mrs. Burns, her daughter," I lowered my voice so only Rose and Daniels could hear me, "…and the missing girls." Silence filled the air. The two of them exhaled, and then looked away from each other. I gestured for Rose and Daniels to walk with me. I wanted to tell them something, but away from Nicole. We walked a safe speaking distance.

"We'll need to talk and get on the same page," I said. "Rose, we need to know more about your investigation."

"Black, I'm not at liberty to provide those details, especially to a civilian. You're pushing it as is," she said.

"Well, share what you can, but first things first. Let's get Mrs. Burns somewhere safe."

"We're working on that," Rose replied.

"Wait, I want to handle that," Daniels said. "I don't trust the Bureau."

I saw Rose biting her lip, ready to respond. I raised my hand towards her, signaling for her to stay cool.

"That may actually be a good idea, at least until we can all get on the same page about what's going on. I mean, she has been okay while staying here in the hospital," I said. "So can we all agree that Daniels will take Mrs. Burns someplace safe to stay with relatives while we exchange intelligence and try to get a grip on the situation?"

Daniels timidly nodded in agreement while Rose looked at my face then the floor.

"Fine," she said.

"Okay, good. We just need to find a quiet place that the four of us can meet," I said.

"Let me handle that," Rose replied.

"When you say four, who do you mean?" Daniels asked.

"I mean you, Rose, Davis, and myself. You three are the only ones I trust so far."

I noticed a slight tremor in Rose's hand. Clearly she was under a lot of stress trying to keep everything together.

"Okay, so I'd better get going. Give me a few hours to take care of the arrangements for Nicole," Daniels said.

"Okay, I'll fill Davis in then work on finding a meeting place," Rose said.

Daniels nodded then walked towards Nicole. Rose followed behind him.

"Hey, Rose," I called.

Rose turned towards me with her tough facade. "What, Black? You're already swimming in deep water. I know you and Daniels were at the Burns residence earlier."

"I just wanted to let you know everything will be okay, but you have to fill me in."

Rose's facade slowly began to chip away. "Look, Black, this investigation is already a big enough mess. I don't need a civilian getting involved, complicating things or getting hurt."

"Oh I get it, you're concerned about me and you think I'll get hurt," I joked.

"Seriously, Black, this can be very dangerous—and then you have the law. There could be some legal repercussions."

I grabbed her hand and felt the light tremors vibrating through it. "I'll be okay. Don't worry about me. Watch your back. Focus on the investigation and the victims."

The tremors stopped. She exhaled a sigh and stared firmly at my face.

"Black," she said.

Davis was approaching, so I carefully released Rose's hand.

"Lee, what's the plan?" he asked.

"I'll fill you in on the way back to HQ," Rose said while slowly tearing her gaze from my face.

All of us headed out the front entrance of the hospital. Daniels was setting Nicole's tote bag into the back seat of a white Chevy Malibu that was parked behind my car. Daniels' friend was at the wheel. I strolled over and leaned against my car. I peeked over my shoulder and noticed Rose and Davis cutting through the circular driveway into the visitors' parking area.

Daniels stepped up to my car. "Black, I need to get my bag out of the back."

"Oh yeah."

I unlocked and then opened the passenger side door. I stepped a few feet backwards to give Daniels some clearance. He leaned into the car. Nicole walked up to me.

"Mr. Black," she called.

"Yes, ma'am."

"Upstairs I told you that you remind me of the two most important men in my life. I'm sure you know, but one of those men is missing, my husband. He has been missing for almost a month, and now my little girl is missing too. I'm aware you don't know them or me, but my— my... family is all..."

"Mrs. Burns, I... ah..." I struggled for words.

Daniels rose from the car with his bag in hand. "There we go. Ready, Nicole?"

"I'll be there, Pete, give me a minute," Nicole replied.

Daniels looked at Nicole and me. "Okay, I'll be at the car."

"Mr. Black, I'm sorry. It's just that if something happens to my family, I... I don't know what I'd do," she wept.

I fell victim to the desperation she was feeling and had no idea what to say. I could see the fragility in her eyes, a woman who felt she was losing everything. "Look, Mrs. Burns, you should get going. I—I promise everything will be okay." *I promise? Black, what did you just do?*

Nicole smiled then grabbed my hand. "You're right. Thank you."

She then gently broke her grip from my hand and found her way back to the Malibu. She ducked into the front passenger seat. Daniels closed the trunk of the car then waved to me. "Black, I'll be in touch," he said.

"Remember to double back a couple times," I said.

Daniels patted the air between us, signifying he had

everything under control. "Don't worry, I know how to spot and lose a tail, Black."

Yeah, just like you did at the Epic Center, I thought. I watched as the Malibu cruised counterclockwise around the circular driveway and disappeared. I slid under the steering wheel of my car, fired it up, and headed home.

I arrived at my house about thirty minutes later. Everything was quiet and the stakeout car was gone. I backed into the driveway, jumped out of the car, and inspected my yard and the exterior of my house. There was nothing out of the ordinary. Entering through the front door, I scanned the inside and noted that everything was just as I had left it. However, given recent events and the obvious target painted on my back, I concluded that staying at my house for too long wouldn't be a good idea.

I raced to the basement, removed the false wall, opened the locked doors, and accessed the small hidden closet. I grabbed a knife to replace the one I had stuck into Evans' hand and inserted it into the open slit of my right ankle holster. I then pulled a cell phone data transfer device, a spare cell phone, and a charger from the tool box in the closet. The cell phone was a clone of my usual one, but it had a ghost chip installed, making it untraceable. One of the many ways I learned how to go off the radar during my final years with the U.S. government. I plugged the cell phone into the charger and stuck it into an outlet.

In the bedroom, I snatched a small travel sack from the closet and walked over to my dresser. From the top drawer I removed two pairs of underwear, from the middle drawer two shirts, and from the bottom drawer a pair of jeans. I stuffed them all into the travel sack then followed them with a bar of deodorant, a tube of toothpaste, and my toothbrush from the bathroom. I zipped it up and walked to the living room. I peeked out of the window then laid the sack next to the front door.

Then I returned to the living room and lounged into my chair. I relaxed my neck, letting my head fall back as I sighed into my thoughts. I really didn't want to get involved, but that didn't matter anymore, because they were coming after me—so I was involved, whether I liked it or not. I knew I could do something about it, so I decided that I would. After all, I had made a promise and I planned to keep it; now it was more bad luck for the bad guys than for me. I built a visual chess board in my mind and could picture most of the players on the board: myself, my enemies, allies, victims, potential enemies, and potential allies. The board was clearer to me than it had been the day before. I saw clearly the next few moves I should make.

One of the problems, though, was that I only had hunches and possibilities as to how it all tied together. I knew there was a bigger player involved—someone pulling the strings—I just didn't know who. I needed to get more information about that Asian guy I had seen with Bennett. I figured I'd try to get that information from Rose and Davis later, if they even knew anything. I hadn't seen his face in their little binder. I dug in my pocket and retrieved the key chain I had taken from the twin at Burns' house. The key chain jingled with a brass sound. I sat up straight and removed the key for the Chevy vehicle from the key ring and put it in my pocket. I carefully studied the small key, which I was almost certain was a key for a post office box. I put all the keys back in my pocket.

"Hmm..." I sighed.

My head swung back again and my body settled deeper into the chair. I dozed off for a spell, still very aware of what was going on around me. I heard the wind blow a whistling breeze between the trees and brushes. I heard the birds chirp a song in a near perfectly composed symphony. The sound of the wood in the house expanding under the sun's heat slowly shredded in my ears.

I remained in this state for about one hour before I leaned

forward, stood from my chair, and stretched. I walked back down to the basement and picked up the spare cell phone with the ghost chip. It was bordering on one hundred percent charged, so I attached it to the data transfer device then took the cell phone from my coat pocket and also plugged it into the device. My goal was to transfer everything from my previous phone onto the phone with the ghost chip. I poked a few keys and the transfer began. It didn't take long because I don't keep much info on my phone. All that social media stuff, showing what you do every waking moment of the day, is not for me. I consider taking twenty pictures of myself then choosing the one I think looks the best to be a lie. Apps for how to tie your shoes and constant texting are not for me. They have their place and I treat them as tools, but I could definitely live without them. It's another way I've learned how to go off the radar and become invisible.

With the data transfer completed, I scrolled through the phone with the ghost chip. Everything was in order. It was an exact duplicate of my other phone. I detached both from the transfer device, then took it to the closet and placed it back into the tool box. From the tool box I also pulled a small lock pick kit and placed it in my inside coat pocket. Next, I grabbed some cash and stuffed it in my wallet. Finally, I closed and locked the doors leading into the closet and replaced the false wall.

The cell phone with the ghost chip went into my coat pocket, while the previous cell phone got turned off and, along with the charger, went into the travel sack near the front door. I thought for a second and figured it would be a good idea to test the cell phone with the ghost chip before I left the house. I reached for my pocket but before I even reached it, felt the vibration from an incoming call against my chest.

The phone number was one I was familiar with, because I had committed it to memory. A smile shaped on my face. One reason was because it was Rose calling, and I was looking forward to hearing her voice; the other reason was that the data transfer seemed to be working nicely. I tapped the answer button.

"Hello," I answered.

"Hi, Black," Rose replied.

I could hear her smile through the phone.

"I know where I want us to meet. It's a place in south Charlotte," and she gave me the address. I was familiar with the area. It was a pretty busy location. I didn't think it would be ideal, but I didn't want to argue with her.

"Okay, have you let Daniels know yet?"

"No, not yet. If you have his number can you relay the information to him?"

I concluded that it would be a good chance to test the outbound calling functionality of the phone. "Sure," I replied. "About what time would you like to meet there?"

"I'm thinking an hour and a half or so," she said.

"Okay, I'll let him know."

"Okay, see you then, Black. Bye, until then."

"Rose, wait," I said. "Watch your back, okay?"

"Thanks, Black, but I can take care of myself. It's you, the civilian, I'm more concerned about. Make sure you watch your own back."

"Fair enough, bye."

"Bye."

Rose's voice vanished into digital void followed by two pulsing beeps indicating the call had ended.

CHAPTER
TEN

I quickly dialed Daniels' number. The phone rang once, twice, three times, four times, and then Daniels' voice scrambled onto the line.

"Hello," he answered.

"This is Black. How are you making out?"

"We dropped Nicole off, and I'm heading back home to pick up my car."

"Okay, when you get your car and you're alone, call me back so I can give you the meeting location. Rose wants to meet in an hour and twenty-five minutes or so, and the location is in south Charlotte."

"Okay, I'll let you know."

"Sounds good. Watch your back."

"You too, Black."

I ended the call then picked up my travel sack and walked out the door. I opened the trunk of my car, tossed the bag in, and hit the road.

After driving for a couple of miles I decided to stop and get gas. I pulled into a gas station next to one of the pumps, and then walked across the pavement to the store, where I picked up two bottles of water. At the front register I paid cash for the water and gas.

"Would you like a bag for that, sir?" the cashier asked.

"No, thanks," I replied.

"Okay, enjoy your day, sir," he said.

In less than five minutes I was back on the road, coasting to the meeting location. I calculated that I'd arrive maybe forty-five minutes before time, which was okay with me. I liked to arrive at least thirty minutes early to case out a meeting location when possible.

When I arrived, I saw that the meet was at one of those outdoor malls. It consisted of a number of stores that formed somewhat of a circle, laid out around a food court. Surrounding the outside of the mall was a number of restaurants, small chain establishments, and a lot of parking. I circled the area a couple times before parking. There were a large number of cars parked all over the area. I decided to wait inside my car. My phone buzzed with Daniels' number on the display. I talked with him for a few minutes. It sounded like he was driving. I gave him the meeting location then ended the call. I remained seated in the car and watched as hundreds of people walked from and to the mall toting their phones, lattes, and purses. Back and forward, in and out. I began to drift into my thoughts but was promptly interrupted by a call from Rose.

"Hi there," I answered.

"I have Daniels on the line with us," she said. "Do you see us parked over at the Original Burger?"

"Yes," Daniels replied.

I looked around and saw Rose and Davis sitting in the unmarked car. "Yep, I see you," I confirmed as well.

"Okay, let's drop the call; just follow us."

I hung up the phone as Davis peeled out of the parking lot with Daniels tailing him and me a short distance behind. We zoomed down the road and onto I-77 south towards

Columbia, South Carolina. We drove down the highway for about ten minutes before shooting past Fort Mill. It was another five minutes before we reached a sign that welcomed us to the town of Rock Hill. At the next exit we got off and made a left onto the overpass above the road. We journeyed maybe another one or one and a half miles before turning into a commercial plaza. It was quiet, secluded, and empty. There was a one-story building made of red brick there, with most of its units displaying signs advertising available space for rent. We coasted towards the back of the plaza.

After we parked, Rose and Davis quickly leaped from the car and approached a unit. Daniels stretched from his car and analyzed the area with curiosity. I grabbed Ireland's wallet out of the glove compartment and placed it in my coat pocket before stepping out of my car. Daniels and I met on the sidewalk right in front of the unit and waited a moment in silence while Rose fidgeted with the lock.

"There we go," she said, and then entered the unit with the rest of us following. I locked the door behind me. It was a little dark inside until Rose flipped the light switch. Everyone glanced and roamed around as if it was their first time there —everyone except Rose, that is, who seemed to have been there before. It was a small unit but seemed spacious, since it was completely empty except for a few rolling chairs and a couple of desks. I strolled towards the back.

I heard Daniels asking Rose and Davis, "What's this place?"

"Don't worry about that right now."

Towards the back there was a small bathroom and a back door which I checked to make sure was locked. I walked back towards the front.

"Don't worry. It's safe to talk here," Rose assured me.

I nodded and leaned against one of the tables. Rose had her body pressed against the other table. Davis was posted up against a wall and Daniels was seated in one of the rolling chairs.

"So, first things first. How is Nicole?" Rose asked.

"She's fine. She should be in Atlanta right now," Daniels replied.

"Atlanta? Did you fly there?" I said.

Rose looked at Daniels with her head tilted. "Wait…" she said, frowning. "Daniels, what happened to your neck?"

Daniels rubbed his neck. "Oh it's just a couple bruises… we'll get to that, I guess," he said. "But to answer your question, Black, no, we met some of the Burns family in Greensville."

I thought for a second then shrugged.

Rose sighed, "So we all want to get on the same page here."

Daniels folded his arms and adjusted his body back into the chair.

Rose continued, "As a sign of good faith we'll tell you what we know first. So I'll just jump right into it. About six months ago, Davis and I were assigned a case concerning a local businessman in the Carolinas who owed a lot in taxes, in the millions. The first couple months of the investigation were what you'd expect, but things slowly became more complicated. We discovered he kept company with some individuals who had ties to the criminal underworld, and he slowly started paying down the taxes he owed."

So he owed taxes but he's paying on them, and he keeps company with some shady characters… I thought to myself. Most people know someone who straddles the line between law and crime. At that point in the story I didn't have enough to make any connections. So I just waited for Rose to finish.

Daniels was a bit more eager to get to the point than I was, because he was closer to the case than me—or any of us. "So what? How does this connect to the disappearances of Frank, Madeline, and the other girls?" he asked.

Davis rolled his back from the wall. "That's what we're trying to figure out," he said.

"Look, I know there's a lot of questions and concerns," Rose said. "But let me finish. We did some digging and saw that he had some legit investments, most of which turned out well, so he was able to start paying back what he owed."

I softly shook my head, trying to make some connections.

Rose continued, "Here's the thing: there were other girls missing throughout the Carolinas before your case, Daniels. I believe it was six."

"Seven," Davis corrected her.

"Yeah sorry, seven," Rose said. "Since the start of the investigation we have intel and witnesses that place individuals that we know to be hired guns with this local businessman." She paused. It was the kind of pause that opened the floor for any quick question, comments, or criticisms.

"So what are you saying?" Daniels asked. "Are you saying the two are connected, the missing girls and this guy?"

Rose absorbed the question, then quickly brushed it off with a head tilt and shoulder raise.

"Again, we're still piecing it together," Davis said for her.

Daniels unfolded his arms and sat up in the chair. "I mean, I've been on this case for about two months and I haven't run across any information like this. I'm confused about how it all ties together."

"So does this guy have a name?" I asked.

Rose nodded. "Robert Uchida."

"Uchida? That's Japanese," I remarked.

"Yep," Rose said. "So, what do you guys have to share?" She and Davis both looked at Daniels.

"What?" Daniels said. "You know my story. I started on the case about two months back. Four missing girls, a missing partner, and a missing partner's daughter later, here I am. I've been under the microscope since you guys with the FBI have taken over, so I really don't have much more information to share than that. You'll have to ask me a specific question if you want an answer."

"Okay, why were you at Detective Burns' house earlier?" Rose asked.

Daniels briefly cast his sights on me. "We thought we would find something to help us locate Madeline," he said.

"I'm going to assume you didn't find anything, but the neighbors said there was quite the disturbance. Do you mind elaborating on that?" Rose asked.

"There were four guys that showed up while we were there. There was this giant Asian guy and two other guys, and boy were they fast!"

Both Rose and Davis stood up straighter and looked at one another for a moment.

"Can you describe the other two guys?" Davis asked.

"Well… they were… um… um… fit and toned… and—," Daniels struggled. I could tell he didn't want to offend by saying they were black, so I stepped in.

"They were black, and they appeared to be twins," I said.

Rose shook her head. "No, it can't be them," she said.

"Are you sure?" Davis asked.

"Yes, I'm certain," I replied.

"Why, what's the matter?" Daniels asked.

"Those guys are professional muscle, you two are lucky. But it does explain what happened to your neck, Daniels," Rose replied.

Daniels smiled a half-smile to suggest the situation was handled. "Well, here we are, and we were able to take care of it," he said calmly.

I shook my head, suppressing a chuckle. *We? Did Daniels forget he was almost choked to death?*

Daniels observed my gesture then revised his previous statement. "Well, really Black took care of them."

"Really?" Rose gazed at me with a cocktail of intrigue, confusion, and excitement.

Davis' face was still larded with disbelief. "These guys are some of the toughest," he said.

Rose looked at me with a surprised flirtatious gawk. "Is that true, Black? Did you take care of it?"

I read her eyes and could tell she was turned on by the idea of me "taking care of it." Excitement shined through her expression of surprise.

"I'll believe it when I see it," Davis grumbled.

Daniels stood from the chair. "You should've seen him... he was lightning-fast. I could not keep up. It was like boom, bam, pow, and we were out!"

I disregarded Daniel's commentary. "We were fortunate," I said. "You guys know who they are, so what are their names?"

"The big guy's name is Kane Okamoto," Davis said.

"Okamoto... that name is Japanese too," I said.

Davis nodded.

"The other two are the Kwon twins," Rose said, "Leonard and Leo Kwon. You can tell them apart by their scars. Leonard has a small scar just above his right eye near the center of his forehead, and Leo has a small scar just below his lip above his chin. I have to be honest: If they're here, this must be a bigger deal than we thought."

The room went silent for a spell.

Davis was the first to break the silence. "Daniels, you mentioned there were four guys at Burns' house, so who was the fourth?"

"It was that van driver, the same driver who followed us to the Epic Center yesterday," Daniels answered.

"Followed you?" Rose inquired.

"It was Evans," I clarified. "Brad Evans."

They all turned to me. I continued, "When Daniels and I left the police station yesterday after my... um... voluntary interrogation, I noticed we were being tailed. The driver of the van I later discovered was Evans, after spotting him in your little photo binder at the FBI HQ."

"Why didn't you tell us then, Black?" Rose asked.

"Good question," Davis followed.

I shrugged. "I'm telling you now," I said. "But to make a long story short, Daniels dropped me off at the Epic Center, then Ireland and Smith jumped out of the van and followed me into the Epic Center. They were carrying Beretta M9s."

"How can you be so sure it was Smith and Ireland?" Rose asked.

"You identified them for me in your binder, plus I have Ireland's wallet."

I reached in my pocket, lifted Ireland's wallet out, and handed it to Rose. She inspected the wallet, flipping it back to front and side to side before unfolding it. Davis peeked over her shoulder to take a look at it.

"Smith seemed more seasoned then Ireland. He didn't have a wallet on him. He did, however, mention something about how his employer had ordered him to capture me and take me back to base. I'm guessing his employer is this Uchida guy," I said.

"How did you get that information from him?" Rose asked.

I walked back over to the desk then leaned against it. "I have my ways," I answered. "But anyhow—Evans continued to follow Daniels, but I was able to catch up with Daniels at a nearby donut shop to warn him. We created a diversion, and then lost them."

"Are Ireland and Smith still alive?" Rose asked straightforwardly.

"They were when I left them."

Rose released a light sarcastic chuckle. "I don't know if I'm impressed or disappointed," she said. "You had this information the whole time and didn't share it, Black."

"You can't really blame Black for not telling you everything right away. I mean, you guys do have a leak," Daniels said.

Everyone's attention fixed on Daniels.

"Do we now?" Davis said.

"Yes, and you guys know you do," I said. "Bennett. I saw him entering the coffee shop yesterday morning."

"You did!" Rose and Davis called out in sync.

"Yep, so how long have you had him under investigation?" I asked.

Both Rose and Davis sighed, again in sync.

"Our superiors are telling us to keep it under wraps, but we believe he has some involvement with Uchida, and that's all I can share at this time," Rose said.

"The Bureau," Daniels sighed.

"Ah, shut up," Davis said. "The PD has more crooks working for them than they put behind bars."

"What did you say?"

"You heard me, white boy."

"He's right Daniels," I said. "Before we were tailed from the PD, I noticed Williams rushing into the station. I also noticed that he and Chief Day appeared a little shook before we headed to Burns' house."

"Okay, so what?" Daniels said.

"You don't think it's strange that Williams was transferred around the same time you were investigating the missing girls? I noticed he interjects himself a lot into your business, and I've only known him for one day. If you think about it, I'm sure you can think of other times he's done the same. Keep your eye on Williams and Day. They're involved."

There was another bout of silence while everyone was buried in their thoughts.

I broke the quiet this time. "Oh, Daniels, that tip you got from Maria—what was it, did you ever follow up on it?"

"It was a tip about some girl, but she didn't match the

description of the other girls so I didn't concern myself with it too much," he said.

"Yeah, but what was the description of the girl?" I asked.

"Not sure, because I had other things going on."

"Do me a favor: call Maria and get all the details you can on that tip."

"Sure, now?"

"Yes," I replied.

Daniels dug his phone out of his pocket and walked towards the back of the office unit.

"Rose, you mentioned Uchida had legit investments to help pay the taxes he owed, right?" I asked. "What do those investments consist of?"

"A lot of things, Black, from stocks and bonds to real estate and restaurants," she said.

"What about coffee shops?"

I looked at Rose's face and saw the shine from the light bulb going off in her head. "I believe we did see Don's Coffee as one of his investments," she said. She turned towards Davis. "That'll be a good lead to follow."

"Yep, and before I forget to mention it, I saw Bennett entering Don's Coffee with another guy, an Asian," I said.

"Uchida!" both Rose and Davis exclaimed.

I shrugged, "I'm thinking so."

"Why didn't you ID him from the photos yesterday?" Davis asked.

"He wasn't in the photos," I said.

"Yes, he was, I'm sure of it," Rose said.

I knew I would've remembered seeing him if he was in the photos, I thought. "Do you have the binder with you?"

"No, didn't think we would need it."

"There were a number of photos and it was a long day. You could've overlooked it," Davis said.

Daniels came back over, stuffing his phone back into his pocket. His face carried anguish. "The girl that Maria described from the tip sounded a lot like Madeline. It was a little girl matching her description, at least. She was seen in a dark four-door sedan with two men. One was driving and the other was in the back seat with her. The eyewitness, who was a driver, thought it was strange, so he called it in."

I caught Rose and Davis whispering to one another. Rose appeared to ask Davis a question. He shrugged. Rose then turned her attention towards Daniels and me.

Daniels continued, "The time was close to the time of the break-in, and it was near the NoDa area where Frank's house is."

I saw her early that morning close to where I live, and it wasn't a dark sedan but the black van... It didn't connect, but I thought I'd share the fact that I saw her. I started to speak, but Rose beat me to it.

"I have more to share about yesterday morning," she said. "As you now know, we have Agent Alex Bennett under investigation. Well, we had intel to suggest that he was meeting with Uchida or someone on Uchida's payroll. So we put Garcia and Hogan on his place that night until morning. Garcia and Hogan identified Bennett entering a dark sedan with two other men. They tailed them but they ended up losing them."

"I only saw the black van," I said. "I didn't see a sedan. So it's possible Bennett could have met with Uchida and Evans somewhere and switched rides."

"That's possible," Rose nodded.

I decided not to mention that I saw Madeline, because it really wouldn't help and there was a little guilt and shame on my part. Only a little.

CHAPTER
ELEVEN

As we sat facing each other, me on top of the desk and the three others in chairs, there was palpable tension in the air of the small office unit. Not physical tension, but the tension of thought. We were all trying to connect the dots.

"What does Bennett's position as director of the Office of Whatever consist of?" I asked.

"The director for the Office of Private Sectors," Rose clarified. "The Office of Private Sectors works closely with businesses to ensure the safety of the country. They work together to identify threats to national security."

It was just as I'd expected, because I'd worked with similar departments in the past.

"I'm assuming that the Bureau gives certain incentives for the participation of these businesses?"

"There are some," she replied.

"What about Uchida? How much private property does he own outside of his businesses?" I asked.

"He has land all over the Carolinas," Davis answered. "Charlotte, Raleigh, Asheville, Myrtle Beach, Charleston. The places where he spends the most of his time are Asheville, Charlotte, and Charleston though."

I glanced at Daniels. I could see the worry and fatigue plastered on his face.

"Well, I hope we're all on the same page now," Rose said. "The information gives us a few leads to follow."

Daniels shook his head. "I'm not sure how any of what we just discussed is going to help us find Madeline, Frank, or the missing girls."

"One step at a time," Davis replied.

Daniels stood up from his chair, agitated. "By the time we finish 'stepping' it may be too late! What if they're dead right now because we've been too slow?"

"Calm down. They're not dead," I said. "Burns knows something, or has something, that is threatening to them. That's why they broke into the house to kidnap Madeline—to get him to talk."

The worry and fatigue on Daniels face was wiped away with confusion. "What?"

"How can you be so sure?" Rose asked.

"Well, it's obvious it wasn't a robbery, because all their valuables were left behind. The other thing is, Madeline was seen in a sedan the same morning Bennett was spotted entering a sedan," I explained.

"Okay, I get that," she said.

"Also there's this," I said as I raised the key ring from my pocket. "I got this off one of the Kwon twins."

Rose sprang from her chair, reaching for the key ring. I extended my hand to meet her halfway.

"What is it?" she asked eagerly.

"It's Burns' house key and a smaller key that I believe goes to some type of P.O. box." I said. "Does Burns have a P.O. box? And did anyone from either the PD or FBI check it?"

"I didn't think to check that," Daniels said.

"He does and we checked it," Rose answered. "There was nothing of importance, just junk mail mainly. But there was something strange. There was a manila envelope with no return address and blank sheets of paper inside it. We started to track where it came from, but pushed it to the back burner because all of the other stuff we had going on. I'm happy you mentioned it, Black. I forgot it."

"The 'to' address, was it a sticker or handwritten?" I asked.

"It was handwritten."

"Have you guys had a forensic document examiner take a look at the handwriting?"

"Not yet. We were tracking it but got pulled into other things," Rose repeated. "We'll follow up on that."

We all stood.

"Well, I think this was a very productive meeting... good idea, Black," Rose continued. "You both were very helpful, but we'll take it from here."

"What do you mean? I want to help," Daniels protested.

"Look, Daniels, let us take care of this, okay? You're too close to this, and Black is a civilian."

"I'm fine. I can do something..." Daniels said. "And you think Black is just a civilian? It doesn't take much to see he's had some training."

"I know, Daniels, but there are laws, you know. So that's why I'm saying officially that you don't have my blessing. Unofficially, you both have my number if you come across something," Rose said.

Daniels smiled and nodded.

"Black, I'll place Garcia and Hogan back at your house tonight."

"No, no need," I replied. "Use them in your investigation. You're going to need all the help you can get."

"But it's dangerous, Black. People are going missing!"

"Trust me, I'm aware of the dangers, probably more than anyone else here. And you're right, people are going missing, but don't be surprised if people start dying soon. They're in cleanup mode, so it's something I've already prepared myself for."

That statement sucked the air out of the room; it went from feeling like an open office to a sealed vault. In that short moment I didn't hear anyone breathe. I didn't hear a single heartbeat. Everyone came into terms with their mortality. No one was exempt from the possibility of death. Not an FBI agent, police officer, civilian... no one.

"For this reason, I think we need to work together and stay on the offense. Meaning that Garcia and Hogan need to be used for the investigation, because I wasn't planning on staying home tonight and neither should any of you. It would be a good idea to find a few different places out of town to stay," I said.

"You make a good point," Davis said.

"I agree, but if you two run into any trouble or notice anything, let us know right away, okay?" Rose instructed Daniels and me.

"Yes, ma'am," I responded, and Daniels nodded.

We exited the unit. It was still daylight outside; it was late afternoon.

"C'mon, Davis, we have a lot of work to do," Rose said.

"Hey, Rose," I called after her. "Watch your back."

She smiled.

Then I called out to Davis and gave him the look a father gives a young man who is taking his daughter out on her first date, conveying that Rose was his responsibility and I was depending on him to keep the both of them safe. Davis read my expression and understood, acknowledging me with half a nod. I really liked Rose. She was one of the few people who pulled at my heartstrings. If something happened to her, there would be a lot of dead men in the Carolinas that day. The two continued to walk towards their car as I turned to Daniels.

"Remember, don't stay home, and wherever you go,

double back three or four times to make sure you're not followed," I advised.

"I got it, Black," Daniels replied. "I plan to do some searching for Madeline, and then I'll head out of town, maybe to Greensboro to a hotel."

"Okay, just watch your back."

I started towards my car and he towards his, but then he stopped and turned back to me. "Hey, Black, what are you going to do?" he asked.

"I got a promise I'm going to try to make good on."

Daniels shrugged then continued towards his car.

I opened my car and slid under the steering wheel. Rose and Davis had already pulled out, and Daniels was about seven seconds behind them. I sat for a moment pondering my next move and the answer hit me within seconds. I pulled out of the commercial plaza parking lot and chased behind Daniels, who had followed the two agents onto I-77 north towards Charlotte. We were all in close proximity for a few minutes, but gradually I fell behind. I continued to cruise for a few more minutes, checking my rearview mirrors just to make sure no one was tailing us. Before entering Charlotte I made a sharp right onto an exit ramp, followed by a left turn at a light. Traffic was beginning to creep onto the roads. I came to a stop, falling behind a short line of cars. I rolled down my windows as I waited. The air was comfortable with a hint of cool. The sun shined brightly; its rays gleamed through the spokes of a roller coaster ride at a nearby theme park. A sudden breeze seeped between the lines of cars and slapped against my face. Then the cars ahead of me moved forward. I hung a left back onto I-77, heading back south towards Colombia. I rolled up the car windows and settled back in the seat and into my thoughts.

I had concluded from the information gathered during the meeting that Charleston would be my next stop. Everything in my mind and my gut was directing me there. I streamed down the highway and made it about four miles outside of Rock Hill due south before I decided to exit off the highway and circle back to make sure I wasn't followed. Then I bumped back on the road and continued south—but not before turning on some of my favorite jazz funk tunes. The car filled with vibrations from saxophones, drums, trumpets, bass guitars, and clarinets. Before I knew it, an hour had passed and I was in Columbia, South Carolina. At this point I decided to jump off the highway and circle back on again.

Shortly afterwards, I was heading east on I-26. Southeast, to be exact. After another hour I made another small detour and filled up on gas, and then was back on the highway racing towards Charleston. Forty-five minutes later, I had the city in my sights, with some residential homes to my right and a few commercial factory buildings to my left. Trees filled all the empty spaces. Further up ahead on my left I could see the Arthur Ravenel Bridge sliding into view. A light shade of darkness began to cover the sky and traffic became heavy. I was on the highway for another five minutes before I exited onto a local road. There were many nice old buildings, but some of the residences were not as nice, instead appearing to be in the process of demolition. I drove past a museum, a few restaurants, and various historic buildings.

It wasn't too long before I entered the French Quarter. My eyes caught a sign with an arrow pointing to my left which read, "Hotel Parking." I bent a left at a light and saw the parking garage entrance to my right for hotel guests. There were a few cars in front of me waiting at the valet parking stand. I really didn't want to let one of them park my car, however, because if they played around and something happened to it I might have to lay hands on the little punks. I removed the Glock that was in the glove compartment and placed it in my coat pocket.

One of the valets drove away with the car that was ahead of me. Excitement burst on the face of the valet who was up next to park my car. He was a young kid, maybe in his late teens or early twenties; he had some muscle definition but didn't really appear to be athletic. I could see he was anticipating driving my Viper, so I thought I'd use that to my advantage, since I hadn't booked a reservation. He was approaching from the sidewalk, so I rolled down the passenger side window.

"Hi, sir, do you have a reservation?" he smiled.

"No, that's the thing. I don't, but I have cash. You guys do have a process for someone in my circumstances, right?" I said.

The valet looked at my car then thought about it for a second. "Yes, sir," he said. "I'll see if I can get you squared away." He pointed down the street about six yards from the hotel entrance. "Just pull up and park over there, sir."

"Thank you," I replied. I pulled forward and parked the car, then jumped out and followed him into the hotel and over to the front desk.

"Sir, wait here a minute. I'll be back," the valet said.

I nodded.

The valet disappeared into a room behind the front desk. I could hear his voice but couldn't make out what he was saying. After a couple minutes a young lady popped out from the room with some papers in her hand. I figured she was the front desk manager. She stopped at a computer monitor on the opposite side of the desk from where I was.

"Hi, sir, how are you today?" she asked.

"I'm well, just a little tired."

She smiled as she moved the computer mouse and viewed the screen. "I understand, sir, we're going to get you situated so hopefully you can get some rest."

The valet walked back out front.

"So it appears we do have a room," the front desk manager said. "Will you be using a debit or credit card?"

"Cash," I said.

She paused for a minute and looked at the monitor, then the papers she had brought from the back room, then back at the computer screen. "Okay," she said slowly. "You'll have to fill out these forms." I looked them over.

"How many nights do you plan to stay?" she asked.

"Only two."

"Okay, if you're using cash it'll be an extra fifty dollars a night for incidentals," she said as she handed me a pen.

"Not a problem."

Money was not a problem, as I had plenty of cash on me. I'm just not big on checks or debit cards and definitely not credit cards.

CHAPTER
TWELVE

I completed the paperwork and paid for the room, and then the front desk manager handed me the key cards, explained all the amenities the hotel offered, and suggested some nearby restaurants.

"Thank you, sir. You're all set," she said. "Just see the valet at the front to park your car."

"Will I have access to my car at any time?"

"Yes, sir, just come to the front and ask the valet at any time."

"Can I get to the garage myself?"

"Oh, yes, sir, of course. You can take the elevator down to the garage. You can get in and out with your key card. You can drive into the garage on this side of the building," she said, pointing towards the side of the building where I'd seen the parking garage entrance.

"Perfect. Thank you," I smiled.

She smiled back. "Enjoy your stay, sir."

I walked out of the hotel and up the sidewalk to my car.

The valet chased behind me. "Sir, I'll park your car for you!"

I thought to myself, *Not a chance, you're far too excited, chump.* But then I thought, ...*What the heck?*

I tossed the kid the key. "You drive. I'm riding with you."

The kid's face oozed excitement. I fell into the passenger seat. The kid jumped in the driver seat, fired up the car, and drove toward the parking garage entrance.

"Hey kid, what's your name?" I asked.

"Tommy," he said.

"Tommy, I'm Orlando. You know, you're a good driver."

"Thank you, sir."

"You can call me Orlando."

Tommy nodded.

We parked and jumped out of the car. I got the key from Tommy, unlocked the trunk, and pulled my travel sack out before closing and locking the car. We took the elevator back up to the lobby, where Tommy jumped out and waved a goodbye.

"See you later, Mr. Orlando," he said.

I continued up in the elevator to the third floor, where my room was. My room had two levels: On the first was the living area, with a sink, microwave, television, couch, and desk, and upstairs were the bed, dresser, and bathroom. I threw the sack and then myself on the bed and lay thinking about where I should start.

It didn't take me long to decide. After resting for a while, I went down to the lobby, where I waited at the front desk for a moment until the manager looked up.

"Hi again," she said.

"Hi. Where's the Don's Coffee shop?"

"Oh... the new coffee shop... it's just a couple of blocks away." She flipped a map of the area onto the countertop. "We're here... and Don's Coffee is here." She drew a line that curved a few times before connecting the two points.

I smiled my thanks and exited through the front entrance.

The night completely coated the sky. I pushed up the sidewalk and through the crowd of shoppers, pedestrians, and tourists. Five minutes later I was inside a crowded coffee shop. Everyone was chatting, sipping drinks, and typing away on their phones. I noticed there were a couple of cameras, one focused on the front door and another aimed at the register counter. One of the baristas saw me staring around.

"Can I help you, sir?"

"Is it always this busy here?" I asked.

A smiled surfaced on her face and her head slowly bobbed from side to side. "It can be," she replied.

"Who's the owner?"

"Donald Felix," she answered. "He's actually in town. He was here earlier, but I think he's under the weather, so he won't be back until tomorrow."

"Oh really? Did he say what time he'll be back?"

"No, but probably sometime in the morning," she replied. "Why, is there an issue?"

I shook my head. "No, I was just curious. He seems to be running a successful business."

"Well, is there anything else I can help you with?"

"What time do you guys open in the morning?"

"Seven a.m.," she said. "Do you need anything else?"

"No, ma'am. Thank you."

I hurried outside, determined that my next step would be to return and hang out for a while the next morning. I wanted to have a conversation with Mr. Felix. I took the next seven minutes to walk back to the hotel and ate some dinner at the hotel's restaurant before heading back to my room, showering, and turning in for the night. It had been a long day.

My eyes opened exactly at 4:23 a.m. I checked my phone, which was charging on the stand next to the bed, and hit the floor to do some push-ups and sit-ups. I concluded my short workout with some tai chi forms and standing meditation. It was eight past six when I finished, and by the time I cleaned up, got dressed, drank multiple cups of fruit water from the dispenser in the lobby, and finished my continental breakfast, it was 6:44. It was enough time for me to go down to the parking garage to check on my car, put the Glock back in the glove compartment, and make it to Don's Coffee at four past seven.

The shop was empty—apparently, I was the first customer. I was about to buy a cup of coffee, but after thinking about it I decided not to. I just grabbed a news-paper from a rack and squatted in a seat where I could easily watch the door. Thirty minutes went by and the occu-pancy of the coffee shop grew, but no sign of Felix. Another hour went by before I decided to stand and stretch. By this time the shop was overflowing with the aroma of stale coffee and the sound of idle chitchat, and there was still no sign of Felix. I continued to wait; eventually I lost track of time, and the afternoon snuck up on me. I decided to walk over to a sandwich shop across the street, making sure I would have a vantage point from which to keep an eye on the coffee shop. After buying a turkey sandwich and a cup of water, I crossed back over to Don's Coffee and reclaimed my same seat. The shop wasn't as busy as it had been earlier.

Just as I started to wonder if I was wasting my time, Felix arrived. I sat and watched him. He looked nervous. Red drops of sweat dewed his face. I hung my head slightly downward and hid my face behind a newspaper so he wouldn't notice me as he rushed behind the counter to the back room. After a matter of minutes he came racing back, carrying a file. I waited until he stepped outside before I laid the newspaper down on the table and followed him. He was jumpy and obviously under some pressure, because he was glancing over his shoulder every ten seconds. The streets were filled with a nice-sized crowd, so it was easy for me to blend in unspotted. I tailed him down the same street which I had walked before. The difference was we were on the opposite side, traveling west.

Felix made a right at the U.S. Custom House and walked maybe twenty yards before crossing the street, then entering the Waterfront Park. As I maintained a safe distance behind, the park welcomed me with polished stone steps circling a water fountain. There weren't many people around, so I fell back a little more in order to remain unnoticed. We glided over the stone paving, which led onto a wooden dock with a magnificent view over the Cooper River. I didn't go onto the dock—Felix made a sudden right through the park. The smooth feel of the stone under my feet had transformed into the rough crunch of small pebbles. Felix was well ahead of me, so I took in the sights as I walked.

To my left was a river that poured out into the ocean. To my right was a small but nice neighborhood park, with well-tended palm trees and flourishing grass. The warm shimmer of the sun mixing with the cool breeze and the smell of grass and water created quite a tranquil experience.

I continued to grit across the pebbles after Felix.

We came up to a medium-sized house that sat back from the river. It was gated all around and on the river side had a dock and a small yacht. The gate was barred, so I could see straight through, up the driveway and to the front door of the house. There was no plaque or sign on the outside of the gate to identify the owner. I made myself invisible behind a tree while I watched Felix poke at the gate keypad, and seconds later it opened. Felix glanced around before passing through and strolling up the driveway. I went to follow him, but I noted a black car snaking around the corner, so I retreated back behind the tree. I watched as the car met Felix close to the front entrance of the house and parked. Two men stepped out, two men with whom I was familiar: Ireland and Smith.

Ireland was wearing a neck brace and Smith walked with a tiny limp. No doubt they were still a bit banged up from our encounter at the Epic Center. The three men talked, sufficiently engrossed in their conversation to allow me to sneak in through the gate and hide behind a pair of shrubs inside. Felix handed the folder to Smith, and a moment later the three jumped in the car and drove onto the street and away. I surveyed the yard and didn't see a sentry, a camera, a dog... nothing. I carefully jogged up the driveway. The front door was locked. I walked to the side of the house and found another door. I tried it, but it too was locked. Looking up, I noticed there was a window slightly cracked above me. I stepped back, ran towards the side of the house, kicked off the wall, and pulled myself up by the window ledge. I pried the window open and dropped into a bedroom.

The house was quiet. I crept out of the room and into the living room, where I noticed a piece of mail on a table. The envelope was from the electric company and addressed to Robert Uchida. I memorized the address on it before quietly sneaking throughout the house, which I found to be clean and well furnished. I passed through the kitchen and checked in a bathroom, another bedroom, and a study. They were all empty.

I really wanted to find Burns in the house. I may have even whispered the words "Detective Burns" a few times, in hopes he would answer. I circled back into the living room. There was a hallway on the other side of the house I hadn't checked. Before I could make my way down the hall, however, the sound of the front door opening filled the living room. I ducked into a nearby closet, lightly closing the door. It was a louver door, so I could peek out from between the slats.

Felix came dragging into the living room with concern splattered on his face. Smith and Ireland were behind him.

"All of it's there! Che— check the paperwork," Felix protested.

Smith was shaking his head. "Don, Don, Don. This isn't the first time the boss has had to check the books behind you.

We even had to go back to the coffee shop just to make sure you had all the paperwork."

"But it's there… Just take it to him!"

Smith walked over and put his arm around Felix's shoulder, "Look, Don, I have orders from upstairs to take you and the girls to Sully Island."

Girls? I thought, immediately drawing a connection.

"Bennett will be looking over the files, because you know we don't know what all these numbers mean," Smith said. He looked around, "Where are the girls?" he added.

"I think the little tramps are out back near the pool," Ireland answered.

"Well, go get them so we can get ready to go."

Ireland left the living room by the hallway I hadn't gotten a chance to check.

"So… wh— what do you think will happen to me?" Felix asked timidly.

Smith shrugged his shoulders. "If everything is straight like you say it is, you should be fine, right?"

Felix stared at the floor. "Mr. Uchida is making a killing, I… I mean with these two girls alone he'll make maybe a one and a half, two million-dollar profit. I've cleaned a ton of money for him."

"That's above my pay grade," Smith said, nonchalant.

Ireland stepped back into the living room, soon followed by the voices of girls echoing down the hall. Two young blonde-haired white girls entered the living room. They were very attractive. Nice smiles, nice skin, well groomed—what many would consider beautiful model material.

"Where are we going?" one of the girls asked.

"Where's Robert?" the other questioned.

"You two calm down. That's where we're going… we're going to see Robert," Smith replied.

I squatted in the closet, confused. The girls didn't appear

to be hurt or held against their will. There were no restraints in sight.

"Now get your things, and let's go," Smith said.

The second girl looked at the first. "I don't want to go. I'm waiting here for Robert."

Ireland shook his head in frustration. "You little tramps are more trouble than you're worth," he muttered.

Everyone moved their focus to Ireland.

"What did you say?" the first girl said.

Ireland walked up to her until his face was within kissing distance. "You heard me, you little gold-digging slut," he spat.

"Well, wait until Robert hears about this," the girl replied.

Smith threw a strong glare of disapproval at Ireland. "Look, princesses," he pled. "Robert wants us to take you to Sully Island, okay?"

"Well he didn't tell us that, so I'm calling him."

"Wait, wait, I'll call him," Smith said. Smith removed his cell phone from his pocket and jabbed at it with his index finger. The first girl placed her hands on her hips, the second girl folded her arms, Felix was distracted in his thoughts, Ireland rooted himself in a chair, and I continued to observe, trying to make sense of the situation.

"Hi boss, it's Craig," Smith said. "The girls want to talk with you."

The first girl walked over and took the phone from Smith. "Where are you?" she asked as she walked back down the hall.

The second girl followed behind her. "What's he saying?" she asked.

Their voices faded into the void between the halls.

"They're more painful than hemorrhoids," Ireland said.

"How do you know… you have hemorrhoids?" Smith chuckled. He then stepped close to Ireland, who looked up at him from the chair. "Just remember, with the buyers we have these little hemorrhoids are worth millions."

"I still think it would've been easier to tie them up and tape their mouths."

"That's why you don't get paid to think. We tried that before and, trust me, this way is easier and more profitable in the long run," Smith said.

The girls came back from down the hall. "Okay, can't wait to see you... Bye, babe," the first girl said excitedly. She then pitched the phone to Smith. "Okay, we're getting our things," she declared.

Both girls paraded back down the hallway, loudly celebrating as they went.

"He's flying us to Europe!" the second girl screamed.

CHAPTER
THIRTEEN

Felix, Smith, and Ireland settled in the living room to wait for the girls. Smith was sitting on the arm of the couch facing the hallway, looking in Felix's direction. Felix stood a couple feet away and Ireland was sitting in a chair on the opposite side of the room, close to my closet. I wanted to make a move but was conflicted. The girls were clearly being deceived about their circumstances and relationship to Uchida. If I took out Smith, Ireland, and Felix, then I would've had to convince them of what really was going on. Or there was the possibility the girls would actually help the three of them take me out. I didn't have the patience for either of those scenarios, so I remained quiet and decided the best move was to wait.

"S— so are both Uchida and Bennett in Sully Island right now?" Felix asked.

"I guess you'll see soon," Smith said.

"Was he there when you guys left?" Felix said. "You guys did take that detective's daughter there yesterday, right?"

"Now, that's above *your* pay grade," Smith replied.

I was tired of hiding and I wanted answers. What I had working in my favor was the element of surprise. Ireland was the closest to the closet, so I figured I would take him out first, then Smith. Felix wouldn't be much of a threat, so I'd use him for information. Before I could make my move, it was disrupted—someone else beat me to it.

Smith looked over his shoulder to Ireland to ask a question. "What's taking the girls so long?"

While Smith's attention was divided, Felix charged into him, grabbing his pistol from his shoulder holster. It was a Sig Sauer P with a mini suppressor. Obviously a replacement for the Beretta M9 I tossed at the Epic Center.

Smith rolled back over the couch then onto the floor.

Ireland quickly jumped from his chair and reached for his pistol, but Felix was already in position with the Sig aimed at him. The gun shook under his nervous twitch.

I guess Felix can handle himself, a little bit at least... I thought.

Ireland froze and then carefully lifted his hands while Smith slowly stumbled back to his feet.

"I'm not going anywhere," Felix said firmly. "I'll tell you what's going to happen. You're going to take the girls with you and tell them you weren't able to bring me."

Smith blew out a nervous laugh. "We can't do that, Don," he said.

"You can and you will," Felix replied.

The girls must have heard the fuss, because they were running from down the hall.

"What's going on?" the first girl said.

The second girl released a deep, loud gasp when she saw the gun bouncing in Felix's hand. Then a mistake was made— a mistake that cost the bungler his life.

Felix placed his attention on the girls and swung the gun in their direction. Smith rushed him and the two struggled hand-to-hand, making Felix drop the gun. The girls ducked down, screaming, while Ireland unholstered his pistol, which was identical to the one Felix had just fumbled. Felix managed to wrestle Smith off and reached down, snagged the dropped pistol, and swung it upward with both hands. He aimed it at Smith, but too late. Ireland squeezed the trigger first. The sound was muffled by the suppressor, but it was still loud, like a balloon pop. The bullet pierced through the air and into Felix's left temple. His body hit the ground even before his gun did.

Smith staggered over him, panting, shocked about what had just happened. The girls collapsed on the floor near the hallway, weeping and crying in fear. Ireland lowered his gun, confused about what had just happened; he had acted from pure instinct, high on adrenaline. Now he slowly fell from that high and lowered the gun all the way down to his side.

Smith looked back at him angrily. "Now, why'd ya go and do that?!"

Ireland's face was of total disbelief. "I... I thought... h— he was gonna kill you," Ireland stuttered.

"Well, I guess we'll never know now," Smith responded. "Let's just clean this up. We have the paperwork so we should be fine. We'll just say he was trying to play with the merchandise here."

The first girl wiped her face. "Merchandise? Wha— what's going on? I want to talk to Robert!" she cried.

"You'll talk to him soon enough," Smith said.

"He murdered him!" the second girl shouted. She stood up and marched for the front door, proclaiming, "I want to go now."

Smith grabbed her arm. "You'll have to wait here in the house, okay?" he said.

The girl pulled against his grip. "No, I don't want to!" she cried.

Smith yanked her arm, and both of the girls screamed. The first girl tried to break Smith's clamp around the other girl's arm. There was tugging, fighting, and screaming.

Ireland raised his gun. "You whores sit down now!" he yelled.

The girls paused, Smith released his grip, and the girls

quickly crawled back to the floor. It was obvious Smith was tired of being diplomatic. He towered over the girls.

"We own you, and you'll do what we say when we tell you, understand?!" he roared.

"I want to talk to Robert," the first girl sniffled.

Smith snickered. "You actually think he cares about you? He was using you. He's had a few of you... you may be going to Europe, but he isn't going with you, sweetheart."

"So there's no entertainment work in Paris?"

"Sure there is, but you'll be entertaining in a different way," Ireland said.

I'd heard and seen enough. I turned the doorknob and pushed the door violently, sending it off its hinges to crash against the wall. Smith stood stiff with his mouth gaping open, Ireland turned white, his eyes wide, and the girls looked both surprised and confused—but mainly confused.

Ireland tried to swing his gun around towards me, but I was already on him. I grabbed the hand holding the gun as he was still turning his body and I bent his wrist backwards to loosen his grasp. He let the gun go but not before a round was sent splitting into the floor between us. The gun bounced off the hardwood floor and slid under the couch. He screeched in pain as I pushed his wrist downward, his fingers pressed almost to his forearm.

Meanwhile, Smith tripped over Felix's corpse trying to get to his gun.

I quickly delivered an elbow to Ireland's neck, smashing into his neck brace. He howled in agony, his body banging against the wall.

Smith reached down and clutched his gun with one hand, planning to aim it in my direction. But he had two problems. Problem number one: I was no longer where he thought I was. Problem number two: He couldn't move the gun because the heel of my boot was firmly pressed against the center of his hand as it lay over the gun.

A grin crossed my face as Smith looked up at me, then the heel of my other boot stumped flush against his face. He tumbled backwards and lost his footing, smacking his back onto the floor. He almost landed on the girls, but the two scurried aside.

Ireland appeared to be resting against the wall for the moment, but I saw his hand drifting down his shin. He was reaching for his ankle piece.

I raced towards him in quick strides, the fastest I had made in a long time. He removed his side piece from its ankle holster, but only by the tip of his fingers—he didn't have firm control of the gun. He cried as I kicked his hand against his shin. The small Glock 43 fell to the floor as I quickly followed up with a right side kick to his stomach. His whole body hunched inward around my kick, the force knocking him back then rolling him across the floor towards the front door.

I heard one of the girls scream, "Stay away from me!"

I turned and saw Smith carefully inching towards the two girls. He was being very careful because the one in front was pointing his gun at him.

Smith noticed my attention on him and panicked. "Give me that, you little tramp!" he yelled out.

He jumped at the girls, but was met with a bullet. The first round popped through the suppressor, entering into his gut. Smith palmed his stomach in disbelief and continued charging towards the girls. The girl fired a second round, then five more in quick succession. It sounded like six hard but muffled knocks at the door. Smith dropped to his knees and fell flat on his face.

The girl continued squeezing away at the trigger, but the gun was empty. The trigger's clicking sound and frantic cries from the girls filled the space of the living room. I dashed towards the two, carefully stepping over Smith's body, which lay just a few feet away from Felix's. The girl was still holding the gun, now aiming at me.

I put up my hands. "Hold it. It's okay," I said.

She dropped the gun then began to cry while the other girl hugged her with tears running down her cheeks. I could hear the door open and I knew it was Ireland, but I couldn't see him because there was a wall in my line of sight. As I ran after him, I heard the door close. Before turning the corner, I looked back at the girls.

"Call your parents, then the police. Tell them exactly what happened, okay?!"

The two girls nodded somberly in understanding.

Outside, Ireland was fighting with the door handle of the car he and Smith had arrived in. He realized at that moment that it was locked and Smith had the key. He banged on the car in frustration then glanced back at the house. I was standing in the front door of the house.

He saw me as I drew a slight smile across my face. It was a smile of torment. I wanted him to know I had him and he was finished. Seeing my face, he knew it was just a matter of time. In desperation, he pushed off the car with both palms and galloped down the driveway towards the gate entrance. I chased behind him, but he was fast, making it to the gate before I made it past the car. The gate automatically opened and he veered left. I pursued about seven or eight yards behind him, give or take.

We were running on the sidewalk through the neighborhood. There was a small park to our left and a cobblestone street with parked cars to our right. Across the street was a line of brick condos. He turned to look over his shoulder at me and nearly stumbled over a couple walking to the parking lot on the left. We dashed down the street for another five seconds before he cut left. The distance between us was slowly shrinking. We continued down the sidewalk, dodging, evading, and shoving through the traffic of walkers, runners, cyclists, and vehicles for at least a half a mile. I could see the effort was beginning to take a toll on him. He was slowing down and I could hear him panting from yards back. I was okay. The run felt just as natural as walking to me.

It wasn't long before a cool breeze from the left struck my face with the smell of water. To the left was an inlet that connected to Charleston Harbor. The sidewalk was about six feet above the level of the water. The sky was clear and blue and the sun sparkled off the water. I could see a few sailboats floating along the waves. It was an elegant sight, but I didn't have time to take it all in.

Ireland knocked down what appeared to be a tour guide. I figured this because she was surrounded by a group, all carrying pamphlets, and she was pointing and speaking before her backside hit the sidewalk. I sidestepped through the group.

"Sorry! Excuse me!" I said.

After another four-minute stride, Ireland's pace fell to a jog. I was only a couple yards behind him by then. He noticed the distance between us was quickly decreasing and jumped off the sidewalk, darting across the street. I hopped down too, like a hound on his tail. He cut through a park and we passed a statue with two old-school cannons on either side of it. Through trees, past more statues, Ireland trotted straight ahead. Suddenly he cut left across the grass, nearly crashing into a tree before he crossed the two-lane street.

Once again we were on a sidewalk, but this one had a steep slant downward towards the street. I had an idea—I pulled back from him just a little. He kept peering over his shoulder at me. I was starting to sweat a little, but I still felt okay. I could keep running for miles. A breeze wafted from over the Ashley River on my left. It was so refreshing, it cooled my entire body. After what felt like another mile, his jog degraded to nearly a speed walk. I decided it was time to catch him and get some answers. I could've caught him earlier, but I wanted him tired. When people are tired, it's easier to interrogate them.

I closed the distance between us until we were within arm's length of each other. When he noticed that I was on him, he caught his second wind and burst into a sprint, skipping off the sidewalk onto the street. It was a short-lived attempt; a large SUV, driving at a moderate speed, smacked into him. The tires of the SUV screeched and the vehicle slingshot forward then back as it came to a stop. I quickly slid to a halt, facing the side of the SUV. Ireland soared through the air, slammed onto the asphalt, and tumbled a few somersaults before he stopped. The driver of the SUV held both hands up over her mouth and glared out the windshield, processing what had occurred. I signaled for her to hold tight and remain calm while I jogged over to Ireland, who I was surprised to find was coherent. His leg was damaged, probably broken, but considering the impact, I'd say he was fortunate.

He glanced up at me, crying in pain.

"Today is just not your day, huh?" I said coldly. "Now tell me what's at Sully Island."

He panted, "I'm not telling you squat."

He was a little tougher than I'd given him credit for. I thought that after the long run and being hit by a car he'd be ready to squeal... It didn't matter. I pressed on his hurt leg with my foot, and he wailed in pain.

"Aaahh! Okay, okay, okay!" he cried.

The lady exited the SUV but stood behind the door and called, "Is— is he okay?"

"Yes, ma'am, but I think he has a broken leg. Can you call 9-1-1?"

The lady nodded.

"Wait, wait, no cops," Ireland insisted.

"Wait one second, ma'am," I signaled to the lady.

"Oww... Look, all I know is we were going to Sully Island to meet Robert."

"What time, and where in Sully Island were you meeting?"

"I don't know… Aah… It's at the southwest corner of the island past the lighthouse. It's hard to miss."

"And the time?"

"At six tonight… Look, that's all I know."

We began to slowly draw a crowd, and we weren't very far from a Coast Guard base, so I needed to finish my questions.

"Is that where Detective Burns is being held?"

"I don't know," Ireland answered.

I raised my foot above his hurt leg.

"Wait! Yeah, yeah, yeah, h— he's there in some warehouse-looking building on the island."

I knelt down over him. "You're hurt, so it won't be hard to find you in the hospital. Your information better check out."

"Man, screw you, I told you the truth."

I delivered a quick jab just above his nose. My top two knuckles struck the bridge between his nose and his forehead. His head flipped back then bounced against the pavement. He was out cold.

I stood. "Ma'am, he passed out. Did you call 9-1-1 yet?" I said.

The woman was still in shock, "I-I'm calling now," she said.

The lady thumbed her phone, brushed her hair behind her ear, and then put the phone to her ear. A few cars stopped and a crowd of people began to form.

I walked through the circle of people saying, "Is there a doctor? He passed out," while some individuals ran over to Ireland to check on him. I continued unhindered through the pack and away from the scene.

CHAPTER
FOURTEEN

I walked back to the gated house and stood observing the few police squad cars in the driveway. I figured with the local PD snooping around, it would be a good time to check out of the hotel, so I crossed through the waterfront park, turned left at the U.S. Custom House, and traveled up the street all the way to the hotel. The air was cool and the late afternoon sun was tepid.

I rode the elevator up to my room, collected all my things, and then rode the elevator all the way down to the parking garage. I tossed my travel sack in my trunk and dropped into the driver seat, then cruised out of the garage to the front of the hotel. I saw Tommy outside. He was talking to another valet. I waved for his attention and handed him my room key cards to take to the front desk, as well as some cash for a tip.

I drove off, immediately phoning Daniels. Since he didn't answer, I tried Rose next.

"Special Agent Lee," Rose answered.

"It's Black," I replied.

"Oh... Hi, Black."

"Hi," I said. "Have you heard from Daniels?"

"No, I haven't, what's going on?"

"I think I know where Burns is."

"What? Really… How?"

"I had a run-in with Felix, Smith, and Ireland. There's no time to get into all the specifics, but Felix and Smith are dead."

"What?!… O— okay… Di— did you do it?"

"No, I didn't," I said. "Felix was scared, so he took Smith's gun, and then Ireland shot Felix. It was a very strange sequence of events."

Rose sighed into the phone. "Okay, Black, where are you?"

"I'm leaving Charleston on my way to Sully Island."

"What's there?"

"That's where I believe Burns is. I got it from Ireland that he and Smith were supposed to take Felix and the two girls to Sully Island to meet up with Bennett and Uchida at six tonight."

"Wait, girls? You found the girls?"

"There were two young blondes there. I know it's a lot to digest, but it's a little after four and they're set to meet at six. I'll have to fill you in on the specifics later. Do you have a pen and paper?"

"Yes," Rose replied.

I gave her the address of the gated house. "That's where it all happened. The girls are probably with the police as we speak. How fast can you get down here?"

I heard Davis' voice in the background.

"Hold on, Black," Rose said.

Silence hissed over the line for a few moments.

Rose's voice cracked back on the line. "Black, one of Davis' Coast Guard buddies mentioned there was an accident near their base. There was someone who fits the description of Ireland being taken to the hospital."

"Yeah, about that…"

"Oh my goodness, Black."

"Not my fault. He got himself hit by a car."

"Ahh... It doesn't matter right now, where are you going now?"

"I told you, on my way to Sully Island. Ireland mentioned the meeting place was at the southwest corner of the island past some lighthouse. He also mentioned Burns is being held at some warehouse-type building out there."

"Okay, we're on our way," Rose said. "But it'll be a few hours."

I could hear her fidgeting around.

"Davis is working some of his connections to have the local Coast Guard check out the area. They'll get there before us, but it'll still take a little time," she said.

"I understand, but I want to get there before the meet to make sure Burns is okay."

"Black, you may want to stay low."

"Oh, are you worried about me?"

"I just want you to let us handle this."

"Look, by the time you guys get here it'll be too late. I'm not far away."

"I don't know, Black." Through the phone I could hear Davis' voice and the sound of an elevator opening or closing.

"I could verify it's the correct location. I mean, if you want you can track my phone," I said.

"So you're giving us permission to track your phone?"

"As if you haven't already been tracking Daniels and me."

"Hah... I don't know why you're so adamant about this. I tell you what, go there and see if you can rescue Burns, but, Black, I'm asking you not to engage with Uchida or Bennett. You already have a couple dead bodies floating over your head."

"I promise I'll be on my best behavior. Bye."

"Wait, Black, there's something I want to share. We looked

into the handwriting on the manila envelope we found in Burns' P.O. box. The handwriting belongs to Burns."

"So he sent himself an envelope with blank documents? Why?"

"Not sure yet, but the envelope was mailed from a post office in Charleston. Black, you have quite the nose for this."

"What can I say? I must be half bloodhound."

"I'll see you soon. Please be careful," Rose uttered. I heard the noise of a car door banging shut, followed by a few phone beeps.

I was about a mile away from the Arthur Ravenel Bridge before I turned into a gas station and parked. I jumped out of the car and popped the trunk to retrieve the cell phone without the ghost chip from my travel sack. I hopped back inside the car, powered the phone up, and was back on the road, all within two minutes. I bounced onto the Arthur Ravenel Bridge heading east. I continued east, then south, and in close to twenty minutes I arrived in Sully Island. It was a neat little beach town. There were no skyscrapers, nor many buildings at all, for that matter. There were numerous small establishments. Some looked like they had been houses in the past. The number of residential homes was too plentiful for me to count. People were walking about smiling, happy, with little care in the world, which is common to see in a small beach town, because water can be therapeutic. The amount of wealth it takes to live close to water doesn't hurt either.

There were a few small lighthouses, but there was one that was very large. I thought back to what Ireland said about it being hard to miss. I drove towards it, which took me towards the southwest corner of the island. *So far so good*, I thought.

The acreage around the lighthouse was well kept, and there was a little playground and a few small picnic areas. Beyond the lighthouse was a beach covered with fine white sand. There was a miniature cliff, with a few birds perched on it, and a few people who were using it as a diving board to vault themselves into the shimmery clear blue water. I proceeded up the road a bit past the lighthouse, and soon the road turned into a dead end circle. Beyond the road all I could see were green bushes. I stopped on the circled pavement and stared through the windshield at the green foliage that surrounded me.

And there it was. At the upper arc of the circle to my right was a semi-hidden paved road. It was hard to see if you were far off, but as I pulled closer it became very prominent. There were a number of signs nailed on trees near the road warning me it was private property and not to trespass. *Yes, this has to be it!*

I veered onto the road, which was surrounded with palm trees and multicolor beach roses. My eyes were hit with various colors: green, red, white, pink, and blue. Beyond the palm trees and beach roses there was water on both sides. It felt like an exotic island theme park. The road snaked for a little over a half mile, and what I saw next took me by surprise. The road widened out into a long field with a runway and a hangar. To the left was a beach, with that same fine white sand and shimmery clear blue water, running the length of the runway. Nearly one hundred yards away on the beach I could see a house.

I studied the land and the beach. It was quiet; there was no one else around. I parked on the right side of the hangar close to the trees and bushes, making my car difficult to spot from the road. I picked up the phone, the one without the ghost chip. The time on the phone read 4:47 p.m. The signal strength was at two bars. I placed the phone under the passenger seat of my car and removed the phone with the ghost chip. I observed that this phone had the same signal reading of two bars before I stuck it back into my pocket. I then reached into the glove compartment and removed the Glock.

I carefully edged out of the car. With the Glock in hand, I quickly tiptoed across the grass to the hangar. There was a window on one wall; I peeked through it, and the first thing that caught my attention was the side of a small airplane. One of those private jets. It had something written on the side of it but I couldn't make it out because I could only see a few of the words from my vantage point. The lights inside the hangar were dim, making it difficult to see in. I lightly jogged to another window towards the back of the building. I could make out a small room, but again the darkness made it hard to discern. In the corner there was a figure squirming around in the dark. *I'm certain that's Burns.* I raced towards the front of the hangar and looked into another window, but I couldn't see much more than a couple crates and the front of the airplane parked in the hangar. Outside next to the window was a side door with a key lock. I ran to the front of the hangar and checked the two large sliding doors—also locked. I figured the side door was my best option. I rushed back over to it, sat the Glock in my pocket, and removed the lock pick kit from my pocket. I knelt and struggled at the key lock with the pick. Two minutes later, the lock clicked open victoriously. I gently tugged the door open, and then crept inside the hangar.

The inside of the building was much more spacious than it appeared from the outside. The ceiling was high, and light fixtures and ceiling fans draped from metal beams that covered the width of it. There were a couple of workbenches, one on either side of the hangar's length. There were ladders, jacks, crates, large canisters, and other hangar-worthy gadgets sprinkled around. At the back was a door. I was certain it was the door which led to the room I had looked into. There was also a staircase that went upstairs to another room.

With the Glock in hand, I hurried over the concrete floor

towards the door in the back. Before I made it there, something caught my attention. I slowed down a bit to read the side of the airplane: It had "Carolina Dance" written on the side of it. I shrugged and continued towards the door, but then I noticed something else—a vehicle. It was a small Chevy SUV. I removed the Chevy key out of my pocket, the one I had snagged off one of the Kwon twins at Burns' house. I thumbed the unlock button and the headlights on the SUV flickered once. I nodded. *This has to be Burns' car.* I settled the key back in my pocket then stepped to the back door. I twisted the knob and gently pushed the door open. The figure in the room jumped at the sound. It was a man, but I could hardly make out his face. There was a light switch next to the door. I flicked it on, and the light chased the dimness out of the room.

There in front of me was Detective Frank Burns. He was standing on a worn mattress with his hands cuffed around a pole. His clothes were dingy and torn. He didn't have that same low haircut he had in the picture on Daniels' desk. He was shaggy all around his face, but he had that tough look I saw in the picture. It was lightly overshadowed by a look of confusion as he gazed at me.

"You're Detective Frank Burns?" I asked.

"Yes, who are you?"

"Orlando Black. I'm here to help get you out of here."

I walked over to Burns, placed the Glock in my pocket, and got busy on the handcuffs with my lock pick kit. Burns watched me as I worked, confused.

"So who do you work for?"

"I don't work for anyone."

"So why are you helping me?"

"That's a long story. I'll fill you in later. But now we need to get out of here. They'll probably be here any minute now."

The handcuff link around Burns' right hand sprung loose and Burn swung his arms from around the pole.

"Okay, let's get out of here," I said as I turned towards the door.

"Wait," Burns said.

While he talked I pulled my cell phone out to check the time.

"Thank you for your help, but I can't leave."

The clock on my phone said it was two minutes until five. I placed the phone back in my pocket as I responded to Burns.

"Look Burns, I'm working with your partner Pete Daniels and some agents from the FBI to help get you home safely. So we have to go," I said.

"The FBI, they have a leak," Burns replied.

"Yes, I know, and so does your precinct."

Burns sighed, "I know."

"I'm sure you already know the FBI leak is Bennett, who's on his way here now. They're supposed to meet at six, but I'm sure they'll get here early so there is no telling how much time we have left."

"What, Bennett is coming here?"

"Yes, I got that bit of information from one of their flunkies. Bennett and Uchida will be here by six."

"So they're both coming. No, I can't leave."

"Why not?"

"I heard one of them mention my wife and daughter. I need to know they're okay."

"Maybe you can help answer something for me, Burns. Why are you still alive?"

"What?"

"I mean you're still alive, and you are worried about your family. It seems to me you know or have something they want."

Burns exhaled slowly. "I have some incriminating evidence that links Uchida and Bennett to a case I was working."

"You mean the missing girls case?"

Burns squinted his eyes at me. From the look in his eyes I could tell he was wondering how I knew so much. I could tell he didn't trust me very much either. I couldn't blame him. I still had some rapport building to do.

"Daniels told me about it."

Burns relaxed a little. "Yeah, right… of course."

"So what is it, pictures?"

"Yep, pictures, putting both Uchida and Bennett with the missing girls."

"Okay, so you have digital copies of the pictures, right?"

"No, with some of my investigations I like to stay away from the digital stuff. Makes it too easy to get the device and manipulate the data, which would make evidence inadmissible. I used an old-school film camera and got the pictures developed. Right before they captured me in Charleston, I managed to send the pictures through the mail. I meant to send the negatives too, but I was rushing because I knew I was being followed. So I forgot. When I was captured, they took the negatives from me."

I nodded. "Where did you send the pictures?"

"To my P.O. box in Charlotte."

I shook my head, then walked over and handed him the key to his SUV. "You sent an envelope with blank documents to your P.O. box in Charlotte. The FBI has the other keys that were on your key chain."

Burns glanced at the key before cuffing it in his hand. He then folded his arms. "Look we just met, and I don't trust you. Plus, I don't know if the evidence would even be good enough."

"I don't blame you for not trusting me, but what's wrong with the pictures?"

"Well, it was strange, but the girls were not being forced; they seemed very willing."

"You don't say."

"Enough about the evidence. What about my family? Do you know if my wife and daughter are safe?"

"Well, Nicole is in Georgia with family."

"And Madeline?"

"Honestly, I don't know where she is," I said.

There were a few moments of silence then Burns sank down onto the mattress, shaking his head.

"This is all my fault," he said. "I just had to get to the bottom of this case."

I wasn't good at consoling, so I gave him a few moments.

"This is no time to wallow in pity," I said. "You can do that after this is over."

"This is my little girl we're talking about. I'm not going. I have the element of surprise. I'm going to take a stand and finish this. You can stay or you can go."

"So is your father-in-law just as stubborn as you?" I asked.

Burns gave me a confused look. "What?"

"Colonel Derrick Buckler. Your wife told me the three of us remind her of each other."

Burns chuckled. "No, he is a lot worse."

"I'm getting the feeling that there's no way I'm going to talk you into leaving, so I guess I'm staying too. Like you said, we have the element of surprise. Plus the Coast Guard, FBI, and maybe even the local law enforcement will be on their way here soon. We just need a plan."

Burns looked up at me. "Why are you doing this?"

"I made a promise," I said shortly, then pulled my phone out to call Rose. The time on the phone showed four minutes after five.

"Hmm, now I see where Nicole was coming from."

"Excuse me," I replied as I fiddled with my phone.

"She wasn't talking about just our stubbornness… her old man has the both of us beat in that arena. But the common trait she sees the most between the three of us—you exhibit more of it then both the Colonel and I," he said.

"And what trait might that be?" I asked.

Before Burns could answer, the sound of a vehicle trampling over grass leaked into the room.

I held my hand up towards Burns. "You hear that?"

"Yes," he whispered.

The sound of a second vehicle rolled in just a moment after the first.

CHAPTER
FIFTEEN

It sounded like the vehicles were moving to the opposite side of the hangar from where I had parked. I dropped the phone back into my pocket, then raced out of the room and across the hangar where the sound of the vehicles was coming from. I looked through a window and saw two black sedans. They were parked right at the front corner of the hangar, on the pavement of the runway. From the first car emerged Agent Bennett and the two guys I had seen him with at the FBI office. From the second car Williams slid out from behind the wheel, and Uchida from the other side. *Well, I guess we're out of time,* I thought. I ran back to Burns.

"There's at least five," I said, "Bennett, Uchida, two others, and Officer Williams."

"Williams," Burns said. "I always knew that little punk had something to do with this."

"Well, we have less than two minutes. If they use the hangar sliding doors, we'll still have the element of surprise. If they use the side door we won't."

"Why?"

"I had to pick the lock to get in, so they'll know someone is in here," I said. "Take this." I handed Burns the Glock.

"Wait, what about you?" he asked.

"Don't worry about me, I'll be okay. You just keep your head down."

Burns nodded. The sound of rattling chains rang from the hangar's front sliding doors. Both Burns and I concentrated on the front door for a moment. The sliding doors split open and sunlight illuminated the hangar as dampened chatter traveled to the back of the hangar. Burns took cover behind the wall of the back office room. I lurked towards the other side of the hangar behind Burns' vehicle. Two men entered the building—the two I had seen at the FBI headquarters with Bennett. At first their conversation was faint, but I could make out what they were saying when they had progressed further into the hangar.

"Where are those two idiots? We told them we'll be flying out at six on the dot," one of them said.

"Who knows? They may have been delayed stopping for Felix and the girls," the other one replied.

Then there was silence. Not normal silence, no, not at all. It was the type of silence that was followed by trouble. I peeked over the hood of Burns' SUV and saw one of the men at the side door through which I had entered. He made hand gestures to the other guy, who then walked back to the front doors and waved in the direction of the parked sedans. It was a signal to them that something was off and they had better wait outside. The man at the side door unholstered his gun and produced a suppressor from his pocket which he then began to assemble to his gun. The other man followed suit as he stood at the front sliding doors glaring down the hangar.

"Argh... great," I whispered.

The guy close to the side door made his way down the hangar towards the back room while the other made his way down the opposite side of the hangar towards the SUV, where I was hiding. Both men were checking under the plane and around crates and containers as they made their way towards the back of the hangar. I carefully slid one of the knives from my ankle holster and held it horizontally in my fist. I thought for a second or two, then reholstered it. The more of them we had alive, the more answers we could get at the end of all of this.

I slowly padded towards the back of the SUV and peeked through the back window to the driver's side. The guy walking towards the back room noticed that the door was open and signaled to the other guy, who was at that point just a few yards away from me. Both men turned their attention towards the back room. The guy closest to me started moving away from the SUV and over to the back door at a forty-five degree angle with his gun drawn. I got a look at the gun—a Glock 22.

I had to think fast, because they were going to have Burns surrounded within moments. I started to reach for my knife again, thinking there'd be no way out of this without taking a life. Not that I cared about the bastards' lives, but I wanted to make sure we got the evidence needed for the investigation. I didn't want to make Rose's, the FBI's, or the local authorities' jobs harder with more bodies, but I was definitely not about to break my promise. There was a metal pipe about a yard away from me, and I figured I could use that. But suddenly there was no time for a plan. A gun fired off with a banging noise.

The man closest to Burns shuffled backwards and lost his balance.

I quickly grabbed the metal pipe and ran up behind the guy nearer to me. A second booming sound erupted from the same gun.

The man closest to Burns hit the floor back first and held his leg, screaming in pain.

The guy in front of me was just about to race towards the room until my chrome hollow pipe connected perfectly with the back of his skull, knocking him out cold. I swung it with one hand as if I was wielding a Chinese broadsword. If I'd used two hands like I would with a katana, I might have killed him. The impact sent his gun sliding across the smooth concrete floor of the hangar.

I hurried over to pick up his gun, seeing Burns already on the other guy. He straddled him and delivered a hard, sharp blow to his head. It worked like a high dose of Novocain for the gunshot wound to his leg: It put him to sleep.

Burns picked up the man's gun and placed the small Glock 43 in his own pocket.

I quickly moved towards the window to see what the other three were doing. Bennett was looking around with his gun in hand, while Uchida was doing the same. Williams was pulling something out of the back seat of the second sedan— or more accurately, someone. It was Madeline. I ran back over to the guy I'd hit with the metal pipe, knelt down to take his handcuffs from his belt, and started to tie his hands behind his back. I quickly searched his pockets and retrieved the key.

Burns dashed over towards me, panting, "We did it. We can finish this!"

I latched the cuffs then looked up at Burns. "They have Madeline out there," I said.

Confusion, worry, stress, and fear swelled on Burns' face. "What? No, no, no...," he exhaled.

"Stay calm. Remember they may not know I'm here." I handed him the handcuff key. "Unlock the cuff around your left wrist."

Burns used the key on the restraints around his wrist. The sound of his cuffs hitting the floor and a loud clamor of a voice echoed throughout the hangar.

"Burns, is that you?... I have a gift for you!" the voice mocked.

Burns paced towards the front of the hangar. I ducked behind some canisters and stealthily made my way to the front. I took a look over a crate. Bennett stood at the entrance of the hangar with his gun aimed at Burns.

"Drop it," Bennett said.

Burns dropped the gun, the same gun he had taken from the guy he shot in the leg.

"Daddy!" Madeline screamed. She struggled to move towards Burns but Williams' arm was holding her back.

"It— It's gonna be okay, sweetheart," Burns said.

"Where's my men?" Bennett asked.

Burns shrugged, "I took them out."

"By yourself?" Williams inquired.

"You can't send a boy to do a man's job," Burns responded.

Uchida stepped in view. "Detective Burns," he said. "How did you get out of your cage?"

"Speaking of sending a boy," Burns said.

Uchida holstered his gun then walked up to Burns. "What did you say?"

Burns just gave him a stern look. Uchida smiled then crushed his fist into Burns' stomach. Burns hunched over and coughed for a moment.

"Leave him alone!" Madeline yelled.

Uchida strutted back towards Bennett, Williams, and Madeline, his back toward Burns.

"So, Detective Burns, since we have a young, beautiful guest with us today, for her sake, will you behave and tell us what we need to know?" Uchida said.

"Hey, Robert," Bennett called to Uchida, beckoning him over.

Uchida walked over to Bennett as the latter kept his gun fixed on Burns then leaned forward and whispered into Uchida's ear. After Bennett finished whispering he leaned back, maintaining his aim on Burns. Uchida looked around the field outside. He looked up to the sky for a moment before turning around to face Burns again.

"Is Black here with you?" he asked.

Burns wiped his mouth with the back side of his hand. "You're welcome to go in and check," he said.

"No, we'll try this a different way," Uchida said.

He walked over to Madeline, pulled out his gun, and pointed it at her head. Burns stepped forward automatically, but Bennett kept him at bay with his gun.

"Black!" Uchida shouted. "You have till the count of three to get out here!"

"Wa— wait…" Burns protested.

"I'm not talking to you, Detective Burns. You had your chance to speak. I'm talking to Black now!"

I knew he was bluffing. He didn't know whether I was there for sure.

"One!" Uchida counted.

Yes, it was a bluff, but I couldn't take the chance of something happening to her. Madeline was curled up, tensed in fright.

"Two!" Uchida continued to count. I could see the thick drops of sweat falling from Burns' face.

"Okay, I'm coming out!" I yelled.

I moved from behind the crate and walked up to the front with my hands raised in the air, holding the gun by its trigger guard with my index finger. Uchida ripped the aim of his gun from Madeline and placed it on me.

"Drop the gun," Bennett said.

I carefully squatted to the ground with my hands up then let the gun slide down my fingertip and onto the floor. I stood up straight and continued walking toward the others. The early evening sun beamed on my face as I stepped a few feet outside of the hangar. I stopped about an arm's reach from Burns.

"So you're the Orlando Black I've been hearing so much about the last few days. 'He's too fast, he's too strong, he's too smart, he's superhuman.' I thought they were describing some sort of superhero. But I have to say, you look like a normal black guy to me," Uchida said.

"He's not that tough," Williams said while holding Madeline with one hand and aiming his gun at me with the other.

I stared at Williams hard. "Why don't you come over here and prove that."

Williams smirked.

"Don't be fooled. He has an interesting resume," Bennett said.

As the group of us stood there I got the feeling that something was off. *Just the five of them…*

"So where's the rest of the gang?" I asked.

Uchida chuckled. "While you and Detective Burns were playing around in the hangar, we received a call from one of Bennett's contacts. Apparently a few of the guys won't be attending the meet. But I'm sure you already knew that," Uchida said.

I raised my shoulders in disregard.

"But they were useless anyway, weren't they? They couldn't capture you when asked," Uchida continued.

I said nothing.

"See, we have contacts all over the Carolinas, Black," Uchida said.

"Contacts who don't know how corrupt you are," Burns interrupted.

Uchida walked up to Burns' face. "Money and perception are what my father taught me. You can buy some people, but others, you have to manipulate the way they perceive you," Uchida said.

"What about selling people?" I said. "Did your father teach you that too?"

"And what do you know of that, Black?"

"I know you owe millions in taxes, and I know there were some missing girls on their way here."

Uchida stared at me.

"These girls all fit the same description, am I right? Young... eighteen to twenty-one years old, white, nice skin, blonde hair, beautiful smile. The all-American girl. You went with these girls because of the perception of most of the world. Because of the nonsense that has been propagated for years, most people believe a white woman has more value than most other women. Initially your approach to kidnapping was very aggressive; you probably drugged the girls or even physically harmed them. This was no good, because if you damaged the *merchandise* the buyer would cut your payment. So you opted for a more deceptive method. Flash a few dollars, show the girls a good time, and gain their trust. This was a better approach for the business, am I right? The *merchandise* remains in good condition and it's less suspicious when the girls go missing, considering they leave of their own will. The average detective might blow the case off, considering the girl is legally an adult and left willingly. But I know Burns is not an average detective. He was hot on your trail. So you had to enlist the help of some law enforcement, like Chief Richard Day. This way you had someone inside to keep Burns and Daniels in check. Now, Day looks like the fat, complaining type, so he probably expressed how he needed more manpower, so you had Williams transferred to Day's precinct. This was probably an easy transfer, considering Williams was already on your payroll, I'm thinking. More than likely you already knew you were under investigation by the FBI, hence your connection with Bennett here, who helped you launder the money through your businesses. Speaking of money, it seems like Felix was taking more than his cut. You were probably going to bring him here and kill him, and then dump his body out of the plane on your way to Europe. Your debt, your associates, your companies, and the missing girls are all tied together. Burns knew it, and that's why you kidnapped him and went after his family for the evidence he had on you. But things really started to unravel when the FBI was looking into Burns' disappearance. No one believed that crap about him taking money from a drug bust and disappearing, leaving his family behind. So you had to recruit some outside help, some so-called professionals. Slick operation, but there was a lot you didn't expect. Chiefly, you didn't expect your business to come down my street, and you certainly didn't expect me," I finished boldly, glaring directly into Uchida's eyes.

"He knows too much," Williams said.

"I told you he has an interesting record," Bennett followed.

"It's a shame our business came down your street," Uchida said. "It was due to the incompetence of a couple of people. I believe you two have already met them."

I threw my head back towards the hangar. "Oh, so it was those two who broke into Burns' house... after they dropped Bennett off to meet with you and Evans. I'm guessing you all were going to meet around Don's Coffee after they finished up at Burns' house."

"We did meet at the coffee shop," Uchida said. "But the two idiots let this girl escape before we got there, so we had to go looking around for her. We eventually found her, but it was a pain because the FBI sent the local PD to that area... but as you already know, the PD didn't catch us. They took some suspicious-looking black guy into custody instead."

"You can thank me for that, Black," Williams said. "A black man walking around outside early morning... what's more suspicious than that?"

I moved my gaze from Uchida to Williams, then from Williams to Bennett, to Madeline, to Burns, and finally back to Uchida.

Uchida and Williams had slow-witted looks on their faces. Perhaps they were just surprised that I knew so much, but Bennett seemed to be the most level-headed of the three.

Meanwhile, Madeline was panting in panic and tears were running down her cheeks.

Burns was listening in on the conversation while keeping his eyes on his daughter. It was time for me to start thinking about making a move. I put myself on alert to exploit any opportunities.

"Hmph," Uchida gestured, turning his attention to Burns. "Enough talk," he said.

"I concur," Bennett agreed.

"Where are the photos and information you have? We know you had photos developed," Uchida asked Burns.

Burns briefly glanced over at Madeline. "Didn't you guys check my P.O. box?" he asked.

"You're really going to put this case before your family? Shoot her in the leg," Uchida ordered.

"No, wait! It's at the coffee shop," Burns cried.

"You wouldn't be lying, would you?" Uchida asked.

"No... the file is at Don's Coffee, hidden under one of the tables."

"Okay, this is what's going to happen. Bennett and I will take you with us to the coffee shop. We'll leave Madeline here with Williams. If you're lying, Williams will hurt your precious little girl until you tell us the truth. Or, we may take her for a ride on the *Carolina Dance* there. I'm sure we can get a few dollars for her."

Bennett nodded his head in my direction. "What about him?" he asked.

"Get rid of him," Uchida replied.

"Agreed," Williams interjected.

"Wait, I believe our last orders were to bring him in," Bennett said. "Plus, there are a few guys who'd love to see him."

"Whatever," Uchida said. He then turned his attention to Williams. "Take both of them to the back. We'll close the hangar doors."

I started to scan for any openings I could take advantage of, but with Burns and a little kid to consider, my options were very limited.

Williams shoved Madeline over to me. I caught her with my arms.

"Everything will be okay," I whispered to her.

Bennett used the gun to wave Burns over towards the car. Burns walked in the direction of the car but glanced back at Madeline and me.

Williams pointed his gun at my head. "Move."

I began to turn around with Madeline in my arms.

"Oh yeah, Black…" Uchida began.

I looked over my shoulder in response, still searching for an opening.

"… We'll be checking in with Williams, and if we don't hear from him, a bullet goes in Detective Burns' head. Understood?"

When Uchida finished speaking the air became silent. Everyone was as still as if we were stuck in a painting. We were limiting all of our senses except for one: the sense of sound. A grin hit my face, because what I heard was the sound of opportunity.

CHAPTER
SIXTEEN

The sound of helicopter rotors cut across the air and reverberated through the hangar. Then I saw it, an orange and white helicopter—the Coast Guard. They were coming in from the coast on the far end of the airstrip. Everyone was frozen. There was a moment of silence when everyone was processing exactly what had happened, drawn out a few more seconds by the sound of sirens wailing from the direction of the lighthouse. I quickly forced myself out of the frozen state. I needed to make a move.

Williams was still gaping up at the sky when I rushed him, grabbed the wrist he was holding his gun with, and bent it downward. I used my other hand to make a hammer and smashed his forearm, which loosened his grip on the gun. I took control of it and followed up with a back fist to his jaw. He stumbled backwards. Madeline screamed and covered her head with her arms. The sound of a gun went off just outside of the hangar as I finished Williams with a front thrust kick to his solar plexus. He went flying backwards and slid across the runway.

I took a few steps beyond the sliding doors and saw Burns and Bennett on the other side of one of the sedans battling for

Bennett's gun. Uchida was off to the side, fixated on their scuffle with his gun drawn. I took aim at him. Before I could find a shot, there was a loud smack, followed by a louder bang: In their tussle, Burns and Bennett had smashed onto the hood of the sedan, causing a round to be discharged from the gun. The bullet hit Uchida's center mass, knocking him backwards towards the concrete. After the shot, the gun fell, slid down the hood of the car, and hit the pavement of the runway. I ducked back into the hangar, grabbed Madeline, and carried her behind some crates for cover.

"Stay here!" I commanded.

I ran back out to find Uchida laid out, back against the blacktop, while Williams was holding his side and trying to stand up. Burns and Bennett were still fighting hand to hand. I kicked Uchida's gun away from his body and raced towards Burns and Bennett. I flipped the gun in my hand so that I was holding it by the barrel, dodged around the hood of the sedan, and cracked Bennett in the skull with the butt of the gun. He folded forward to the concrete, knocked out.

"You okay?" I asked Burns.

Burns held his jaw. "Yeah, where's Madeline?"

"She's in the hangar."

Williams wobbled to his feet and hustled towards the beach. The sound of the sirens was approaching—I could see the red and blue lights coming our way. The helicopter was just moments away from us, and the power from the rotors lifted dirt and grass particles from the ground and sent them swirling in a whirlwind.

I handed Burns the gun I had. "I'll take care of Williams; go get your daughter."

Burns hurried into the hangar and I chased after Williams, who was galloping off the airstrip towards the beach. He had a lead on me, but I closed the gap after he tripped and fell. There was a short slope downward from the field to the beach. Williams rolled down the slope, then over and into the powdery white sand. He sat on the ground covered in sand. He shook his head and brushed his face off so that the sand didn't obstruct his vision. I shuffled down the slope towards him. As he saw me coming, he scrambled to his feet and scurried towards the water.

He had fled about knee level into the waves before I snagged him by the back of his shirt. He swung at me with a wild back fist, but I ducked, then hip-tossed him closer to shore. He splashed into the ankle-high water. I waited as he rose to his feet, drenched in saltwater.

"Where are you going? Here's your chance to prove I'm not that tough," I mocked.

He was panting, with anger and water covering his face. "Screw you!" He rushed at me, but ran into my fist with his nose. He stumbled backwards, holding his face as I smiled. He then tried to bum-rush me with a jab followed by a cross. I parried the jab, bobbed under the cross, and then caught him with a light upper cut to the bottom of his jaw. It was child's play. He faltered back. As the Coast Guard helicopter hovered over us, the sand began to tornado and a crater formed in the water around us while deafening noise pushed down at us. Our clothes began to pull and flap in the wind.

"You're done. It's over!" I shouted.

I could see the rage burning up in him. I, the black man he thought would be his scapegoat, turned out to be much more than he'd expected. It was an indubitable fact that he was unequivocally out of his depths. The fact that he lost and couldn't do a thing about it was tearing him up inside.

"Freeze and lift your hands in the air!" the megaphone from the helicopter blasted.

I kept my eyes on Williams and slowly lifted my arms.

Williams was looking down at the water and kept his arms down. I could see the wheels turning in his head as the water dripped off of him. He was thinking about what type of life he would have if he gave up, he was disgusted by the idea of losing to me, and he was struggling with his pride.

"This is your final warning! Put your hands in the air!" the voice over the megaphone said.

"Williams, don't be an idiot. Put your hands up!" I warned.

After a few moments Williams finally looked up at me. He gritted his teeth and reached down under the water towards his ankle. I knew what he was doing. His hand emerged from the water with a shiny small revolver. Droplets of water followed the path of the revolver as he aimed it at me. I dove onto the sand of the beach. Williams' aim attempted to follow me but was intercepted by rounds from the M240D machine gun on the helicopter. He danced as bullets hit his body. Water was splashing all over, sand was bouncing, and the cyclone power from the helicopter rotors was mixing it altogether. His body fell backwards and spattered into the water. I sat there, watching, amazed at how a man could be so arrogant and allow his pride to kill him. It didn't make sense. But then again, if that same man dishonored the badge he carried and participated in the kidnapping and thralldom of young women, how could I expect any of his actions to make sense?

I stood up with my hands raised high in the air. A rope unraveled down from the helicopter. One of the Coast Guardsmen floated down the rope and approached me with his M16 drawn.

"Turn around, put your hands behind your back!" he shouted.

I did as he instructed. He removed a zip tie from his pocket and bound my hands, then escorted me back across the beach, up the slope, and onto the airstrip. The hangar was surrounded by police squad cars. The helicopter hovered over us and began to land further down the runway. The Coast Guardsman walked me over to the hangar. During my approach I saw Burns embracing Madeline. He scanned the field and saw me walking up with the Coast Guardsman behind me. He said something to Madeline, then left her and jogged over to us.

"You can release him. He's one of the good guys," Burns said.

The Coast Guardsman looked Burns up and down. "Sorry, sir, who are you?" he asked.

Burns told him he was an officer and gave him his badge number. The Coast Guardsman cut the zip tie, then stood posted holding his M16 across the front of his body. I brushed the sand off from around my neck, face, and clothes and strolled at Burns' side up to the hangar.

"So I see they didn't put you in handcuffs," I said.

"Oh no, the law enforcement recognized me. I know a lot of these guys. They're not crooked like that weasel Williams. Speaking of which, where is he?" Burns asked.

"He won't be joining us."

Burns thought for a second. "Oh, the machine gun rounds we heard. I thought they were only warning shots."

"Terrible way to go," I said.

"Don't feel sorry for him."

"Trust me, I don't."

One of the officers from the swarm of law enforcement approached us. "Hi, Burns, what do we have here?" he asked.

"Well, we have five perps. Three were injured and two are dead. One is right here in front of the hangar and the other is out near the beach," Burns said.

"Okay, well, we're working on getting the medics and coroner out here. We'll need to get your official statements too," the officer said.

"Okay," Burns replied as the officer walked over to the hangar. "Oh goodie," he sighed to me. "This will be fun to explain."

"Yeah, but I don't think we'll be explaining it to the local PD," I said.

"Why do you say that?"

I pointed my thumb back towards the helicopter. "I think that's our ride."

Two men were walking up the runway. They stopped and talked with the Coast Guardsman—the one who had zip-tied me. Then all three of them walked over to Burns and me. The man in the middle seemed to be in charge. He was a middle-aged white man dressed in military fatigues. Although he was wearing an army bush hat, I could see he had low-cut brown hair with hints of gray sprinkled throughout. He had a hard look on his face and a robust physique.

"Are you Black?" he asked.

"I am."

He extended his hand. "I'm Commander Hicks with the Coast Guard."

I extended my hand to meet his.

"Nice to meet you. I'm a friend of Agents Davis and Lee with the FBI, who filled me in on the situation," he said.

"Same here, thank you for the assist, Commander."

Hicks extended his hand to Burns "And you must be Detective Burns," he said.

"Nice to meet you, Commander," Burns replied.

Commander Hicks and Burns shook hands.

"Agents Davis and Lee are about an hour and a half away from Charleston. I was asked to get you guys back to base for debriefing when they arrive," Hicks said.

I glanced back at the crowd of police officers around the hangar and said, "Okay, sounds like a plan."

Burns looked back towards Madeline. "Is it okay if we drive there?" he asked.

Hicks shrugged. "That's up to you," he said.

I shook my head. "This area is crawling with law enforcement. It'll be extremely difficult to get out of here probably at least for the next couple of hours. You've been gone for nearly a month and you look tired, so let's get you cleaned up, get some food in your stomach, and I'm sure you want to spend time with your daughter and see your wife. We can come back for the vehicles later."

Burns nodded. "Okay, let me get Madeline."

He dashed over to Madeline, who was covered with a small blanket, and led her back over to Hicks and me, but not before exchanging some words with the officer who asked for our statements. The officer listened, looked back in my direction, then nodded and turned his attention back towards someone else.

"All set," Burns said.

"Okay, let's go," Hicks responded.

Burns, Madeline, and I lightly jogged behind Hicks and the two other Coast Guardsmen down the runway towards the helicopter, ducking under the blades as we approached the doors. The wind force created from the circulation of the main rotor tugged at us. Our shirts, coats, pants, and Madeline's blanket waved continuously against the gusts. Burns' and Madeline's hair whipped in the wind as well, but, being a black man, I didn't have that problem. Commander Hicks climbed into the front with the pilot while the rest of us entered through the side doors. The Coast Guardsman shut the door then signaled to the pilot. We covered our ears with headphones, and two minutes later we were eighteen hundred feet in the air. From above, the police squad cars looked like tiny toy cars with flashing red and blue lights. The hangar shrunk to the size of a small tool shed, and the runway was the same proportion as one of those old-school electronic toy race tracks. Most of the nine-minute flight was across water.

I watched Burns and Madeline, seated next to each other. He had his arm around her as if he was planning to never let her go. I felt a smile break across my face. I had kept my promise to his wife. There were a few more loose ends, but they weren't my problem—they were for law enforcement to figure out. The helicopter began to descend towards the landing pad at the Coast Guard base. From the window I could see the exact spot where Ireland had his little accident with the car.

The pilot carefully landed the helicopter and killed the motor, and everyone hopped out. Madeline, Burns, and I were led into the base to a lounge-type room where we found a couple of couches, a few armchairs, a small dining table surrounded by some chairs, and a fridge. On the far end of the room there were some open-access style restrooms, one side for women and the other for men, like what you'd typically see in an airport.

"Okay, you guys can relax here for a bit," Hicks said. "We have some pizza on the way, and there are drinks in the fridge there." To Burns, who was still dressed in the same dirty ripped clothes, he added, "I'll get you a change of clothes and something to wash with."

"Thank you," Burns replied.

Hicks nodded then left the room.

Burns and Madeline planted themselves on one of the couches while I walked towards the fridge, offering to get them drinks.

Burns put his arms around Madeline, who was still wrapped in her blanket, then he whispered something to her. He then looked over to me. "Black, we'll have water if they have it."

I shrugged open the fridge. There were a lot of bottled waters, canned sodas, and some of the stronger stuff. I snatched three water bottles from the top shelf and handed Burns two of them. Walking away, I took out my phone and thumbed Rose's number. After the phone rang a number of times, I was sure I would receive her voicemail.

"Hello!" Rose's voice jumped on the line.

"Hey, it's Black."

"Oh, Black, I've been calling and getting called since we last talked. Is Burns okay?"

"Yep, he's sitting here with his daughter at the Coast Guard base."

"What?! You found his daughter too?"

"Well, she kinda found us, but I'll explain it all later."

"Is she okay?"

"Yes, she's fine. The two are hugged up together now. I'm fine too by the way."

"You always seem to be fine, Black, for some reason. We have a lot to talk about, but I'm getting a lot of calls from the Bureau and the local PD. We should be there in about an hour. Talk to you then. Bye."

The phone call ended before I could respond.

I figured Daniels would want to hear the good news, so I dialed his number but didn't get an answer. *Daniels, where are you?* I walked back over to Burns and Madeline, thinking deeply for a moment.

"Is everything okay?" Burns asked.

I looked over at Madeline. "Yep," I replied. "The FBI will be here soon. Do you want to call your wife to let her know you and Madeline are okay? I'm sure she's worried."

"Oh, yeah yeah yeah, that's a good idea."

I passed my phone to Burns.

Burns typed at the phone, took a deep breath followed by a quick exhale, then held the phone to his ear. He kept the phone to his ear for a few moments before shaking his head.

"No answer. Went to her voicemail," he said. "You mentioned she was in Georgia. I can only think of one place she'd be there, so let me try another number…"

Burns pressed at the phone, cleared his throat, and once again held the phone to his ear. After a few moments he removed the phone from his ear, his eyes squinted and his forehead crinkled.

"No answer from them either," he said.

I knew something was up. If there was only one call made and there was no answer, I would've been okay with that, but that was a total of three calls with no answer—plus, I had called Daniels earlier with no answer. I decided not to jump to conclusions since I didn't want to worry Burns. I reached for the phone.

"Well, they'll see that you called. I'll make sure I keep an eye out for their call back."

Burns handed me the phone with a, "Yeah, sure."

Hicks entered the room. "Here you go," he said, and placed a pair of military fatigues, a white shirt, some soap, rags, and towels into Burns' arms.

"Thanks."

"Happy to help, and there are showers in the bathrooms. I see you guys found something to drink, and the pizza will be here soon," Hicks said just before stepping out of the room.

I relaxed into one of the chairs with my eyes closed. Madeline stretched out on the couch while Burns went to the restroom to clean up. I brought forth that imaginary chess board in my mind. I liked how the board was looking: There were some enemies who had been removed from the board, some victims found, some victims turned to allies, and some newfound allies. Although there were still a few unanswered questions, things were looking up. The enemy's operation was definitely folding. I just wanted to get Burns' family together like I said I would.

I was trying to remain positive. I was hopeful that Nicole or her family would call back. I thought maybe they were out shopping or the family had taken her out for dinner to keep her mind off of things. In regard to Daniels, it was hard to be hopeful, because he'd been distraught about Madeline and Burns' disappearance. *Daniels, I hope you didn't go do something stupid*, I thought.

CHAPTER
SEVENTEEN

Burns returned from the bathroom dressed in the military fatigues and white shirt. He looked neat and his face was brighter. He had his old clothes plus the towel and rag he'd used folded in his arms. He sat them down against the wall next to the bathroom then settled on the couch next to Madeline. I was reclined in the chair with my head tilted slightly backward. Burns spoke to Madeline, and she unwrapped herself from the blanket then walked to the restroom.

Hicks entered the room with two boxes and a roll of paper towels in hand. "I have the pizza," he said. "There's sausage and pepperoni."

He placed the pizza and the roll of paper towels on the dining table. He opened the top box, grabbed a slice of pizza, then slid over to the fridge and removed one of the strong drinks. "Get some grub and rest up. I'll let you know when the FBI gets here," he said while leaving the room.

Burns rose from the couch and stepped over to the dining table. "I'm hungry," he said. "It seems like forever since I've had pizza. Black, you want a slice?"

I allowed my head to relax in his direction then waved my hand to signal I was fine.

"Okay, suit yourself."

He helped himself, and so did Madeline when she returned from the restroom. I rolled my head back and closed my eyes in some much-needed relaxation.

When I opened them again later, I saw Burns sitting on the couch with his head leaning over the back of the couch, mouth cracked open and snoring loudly. Madeline was lying down on the couch covered in the blanket, using her father's lap as a pillow. I sat up in the chair and checked my phone. I had no missed calls and the time showed eighteen past seven in the evening. I'd been sleeping for about one hour. I stood up and stretched, hearing voices coming down the hall. A few seconds later, into the room stepped Rose and Davis, followed by Hicks.

"Look what I found," Hicks said.

Both Rose and Davis looked tired. You could tell they had been doing nothing but working since we last met. Davis was carrying a small suitcase.

"What's good, Black?" he said.

"I am, thanks to you working your connections here," I said. "Hi, Rose."

Rose didn't speak. She only responded with a smile. "How are they?" she asked.

"Stuffed and tired," I responded.

"Well, we need to have a word with you and Burns so we can all be on the same page."

"Okay..." I replied. "Hey, have either of you heard from Daniels yet?"

Both Rose and Davis shrugged and shook their heads.

"Well, let's go," Rose said.

I tapped Burns on his shoulder and he bounced forward from the couch. "What?... Huh?... What?" he blurted.

"Hey, the FBI is here," I said.

Burns stretched and yawned, "Okay." He then carefully

crawled out from under the weight of Madeline without waking her.

"Do you have a place where we can talk privately?" Rose asked Hicks.

"Yeah sure, follow me," Hicks said.

We followed Hicks into the hall. Burns looked back in the room at Madeline.

"She'll be okay," I assured him.

Burns smiled. "I know... hey, Black, did you get a call back from Nicole?"

"No, not yet," I said.

"That's a little strange, don't you think?"

"Give it a little more time," I said. "C'mon, let's get this debrief over with."

Hicks led us to a bunk room. It was more spacious than the bunk rooms I was accustomed to; there were a couple chairs, a moderate-sized sofa, and two bunkbeds.

"Will this do?" Hicks asked.

Rose nodded. "Yes, thanks."

"Holla if you need anything," and Hicks closed the door on his way out.

I sat in one of the chairs, Burns sat in the other, and both Rose and Davis sat on the sofa.

"So, Detective Burns, I'm Special Agent Lee and this is Special Agent Davis," Rose said.

"Nice to meet you two," Burns responded.

"Well, let's get right into it, can you tell us—" Rose started.

"Wait. Wait. Before we start, have you heard from my wife?" Burns asked.

Rose and Davis glanced at me. I softly shook my head.

"No, we haven't recently," Rose answered. "But she should be with family in Georgia. I'm sure we'll hear from her soon. So can you tell us about the events that led up to your capture?"

Burns shifted around in his chair. "Okay," he sighed.

He told us much of what we already knew. He and Daniels had been investigating the case of two missing girls. He had followed a lead to Charleston where he placed the missing girls, Bennett, and Uchida all in the same place. He mentioned he took pictures and had some developed. He knew he was being followed, so he mailed blank documents to himself from the post office but stashed the real evidence in Don's Coffee. He told us he knew at the time that there were leaks in both the PD and FBI, so he wanted to be careful with the evidence. He said the coffee shop would be the last place Uchida would think to check and the pictures were taped underneath one of the tables. He then added that when he was captured, they took his camera and the negatives. He also mentioned how they'd leave him in the hangar alone for sometimes days at a time, and he was happy that I showed up when I did.

"So where did you take these pictures?" Rose asked.

"Where I was held in Sully Island, there's a beach house. I saw everyone at that beach house," Burns replied.

"So why didn't you call it in when you went back into Charleston?" Davis asked.

"Well, the girls didn't appear to be held against their will," Burns said.

"Yeah, that's the same behavior I saw from the girls at that house I followed Felix to," I said. "Apparently they changed their approach to kidnapping. It's less force and more of a wine-and-dine approach."

I then continued on about the specifics of the incidents in the house and everything that led up to Ireland's accident. I continued with what all took place at the hangar and the conversation that took place with Uchida, Bennett, and Williams there.

"Interesting operation," I said, "but they panicked. The pictures alone really weren't enough evidence. If they had never kidnapped Burns, they might've had more time to fix things and smooth out their operation. But their guilt made them panic."

"Well, we've been really busy the last twenty-four hours," Rose said. "So the pictures will not have to stand alone as evidence. After leaving you and Daniels yesterday, Black, we went to work. We checked on some of the businesses Uchida owns and discovered unusually large transactions. We are currently getting a warrant for a full audit on some of those particular businesses."

"Is he a co-owner of Don's Coffee?" Burns asked.

"Nope," Rose said. "But we did see large amounts of money being invested by an angel investor. I'll give you one guess to who that was."

"Uchida," I smiled.

"And with Bennett now an official suspect we'll have access to everything he did while working for the Bureau. I'm sure we'll dig up even more evidence. And there's more. Davis, do you want the honors?" Rose asked.

"Sure. After working our overseas contacts and connections, we're certain we've found the European buyer of the girls. We have surveillance footage of Uchida meeting with him, and eyewitness accounts of girls who fit the description of a few of the missing girls. Apparently this group was already under investigation by Interpol for human trafficking," Davis finished.

"That's great news!" Burns said.

"That's a lot of work in just twenty-four hours," I added.

"I believe someone inspired us," Davis replied.

"We still have a few stops to make," Rose said, moving on.

"Okay… Well, I'm tired. I'm going to check on Madeline," Burns said.

We all stood, and Rose and Davis started a conversation amongst themselves.

Burns shook my hand and thanked me. He then walked out of the room.

Rose and Davis finished their conversation and he handed her the suitcase he was carrying. He stepped out the room with me right behind him.

"Hey, Black," Rose called. "Shut the door for a minute... I want to talk with you."

I closed the door.

Rose reached into the suitcase and removed a file. She stabbed me in my chest with the file. I grabbed it.

"Who are you, Black?" she asked sternly.

I held the file and gazed at her. "You've been asking me that since we met."

"Open the file."

"No need, because you've already made up your mind who I am."

She snatched the file from me, opened it, and then paced around me in an awkward circular path.

"Hmm, orphaned since you were six, you and your little sister traveled around the country from foster home to foster home. You studied kenpo karate, judo, and taekwondo growing up. In high school you wrestled, boxed, kick-boxed, and were in R.O.T.C. Wow, you stayed busy."

"Yeah... Well, it kept me out of trouble."

Rose stopped walking. "Well, Black, it seems trouble always has a way of finding you."

I shrugged. "What are you talking about?"

Rose looked down at the folder. "Your senior year in high school. You mind telling me what that was all about?"

I sighed, "Why would you bring that up?"

"It shows you like getting into trouble more than you want to admit."

"Rose... you obviously don't know everything that happened that day."

Rose continued walking. "Okay, so you went into the military after school... the Army. You didn't spend too much time in the Reserve. You went into infantry and airborne, then spent a few years as an Army Ranger. Let's see... whoa, you were on Delta Force. You received multiple commendations including the Air Medal, the Bronze Star, two Purple Hearts, and, my goodness... the Distinguished Service Cross. You completed your career as a captain. It says you were asked to take the rank of major multiple times but didn't accept. After the military you roamed around Asia for a number of years. However, before that there are a few years unaccounted for. I couldn't find any service record during that time. This leads me to believe the government had you off the books."

I scoffed and shook my head.

Rose paused from walking then looked me in the face. "So tell me, Black. What did you do during those years?"

I looked at her. I could feel the emotion chip from my face. "Things you wouldn't believe and I hope you never have to experience."

The room chilled silent for a moment. There was a sheet of calm that fell over Rose. She became sympathetic to my situations.

"I— I just don't like being lied to," she said.

"I never lied to you."

"You didn't tell me everything... which is the same as lying to me. Here I am worried about your safety, but find out you're a hero who doesn't need my protection."

"I told you from the start not to worry about me."

Rose dropped her head and let out a long, hard sigh.

"When was the last time you were on vacation?" I asked. "This is almost over. Take some time off. You can go catch some sun on a beach somewhere."

Rose looked up at me, smiled, shook her head, and then giggled. I was happy to see her smile.

"I have a lot of running around to do. So we can finish this later," she said.

"Well, if you don't mind I'd like to tag along with you and Davis."

"Oh really? Do you even know where we're going?"

"I know where I would go."

"Please share," Rose smiled.

"First, I'd go to the coffee shop to pick up those pictures and documents Burns stashed. Next I'd check on the kidnapped girls to make sure they're okay and ask them some questions. Then I would probably head over to the hospital, where I'm assuming Ireland and Bennett are being held under arrest. Both should be conscious and able to answer some questions. Then I would go to the morgue to ID the bodies of those who were killed today, to confirm all our stories check out."

Rose stuffed the file back inside the suitcase. "Okay, you can tag along, but I have a few calls I need to make first."

I stood up and walked towards the door, saying, "I need to go to the restroom anyway."

"That's your business." Rose smiled at me as she pulled out her phone.

I walked back over to the lounge room, where I saw Burns and Madeline asleep on the couch. Davis was near the dining table with his phone to his ear in one hand and a slice of pizza in his other hand. I used the restroom, washed my hands, and then planted myself in one of the chairs in the room. I closed my eyes for a few minutes before Rose stepped into the room.

"Okay, you two, let's go," she said to Davis and me.

We followed her out of the room, down the hall, and out the front door. Outside, the sun had set and night was falling upon us. We walked across the concrete driveway to the gate, which was opened for us. Outside was Rose and Davis' unmarked car.

"I'll drive," Rose said.

Davis tossed her the keys. She opened the trunk and laid the suitcase in it before getting in the driver's seat. Davis got in the front passenger side, and I slid into the back. Rose fired up the engine and pulled off.

"Black and I were talking," she said to Davis. "We should go to the coffee shop first and search for those files."

"He mentioned it was taped under one of the tables, right?" Davis asked.

"Yeah, that's what he said," I replied.

We drove for a quiet three or four minutes before parking in front of Don's Coffee. The shop was crawling with people, which was aggravating considering we now knew it was a money laundromat for a human traffic ring. But I contained myself and allowed everyone to continue sipping on their lattes, kissing their cell phones, and making conversation about things they considered important. The three of us looked at each other, trying to determine where to begin.

"Let's split up," I said. "We just need to check under the tables."

Rose started on one side of the shop, Davis on another, and I on a third. I started with the one empty table I had on my side and found nothing. I saw Rose and Davis flashing their badges to get customers to cooperate with the process. I didn't have that luxury. I had to say "Excuse me" a hundred times. None of the tables on my side thus far had anything attached to them. I looked over at Rose and Davis. Both of them gave me a gesture that suggested they weren't finding anything either. I walked over to a table I was familiar with—the one I'd sat in when I was waiting for Felix to show up. I asked the couple who occupied it to allow me to check underneath, and there it was: A manila envelope attached to the bottom.

I ripped the tape from around the envelope then raised it to show Rose and Davis. Rose walked over and I handed her the envelope. She opened it and removed a certain picture from the other documents. Her face beamed.

"This is it," she said.

She took out her phone, snapped a picture of it, then handed the envelope and picture to Davis.

Davis reviewed the picture for a moment then placed it back in the envelope. I never got a look at the picture, and I really didn't care to at that point. We jumped back into the car then swung back around to the Coast Guard base. Rose parked in front of the gate. Davis and I climbed out while Rose rolled down the front passenger-side window.

"Davis, I have to make a couple more stops," she said. "Can you go over the documents with Burns? We need to make sense of everything so we can know what's admissible."

"You sure you don't want me to go with you?" Davis asked.

"No that's okay. I'll take Black with me."

Some alone time with you; I'm down with that, I thought.

Davis walked up to the gate and I jumped in the front passenger seat of the car. The gate slowly drifted open and Davis disappeared behind it. Rose dragged the gear shift into drive and we shot down the road under the cool, dark night sky. I looked over at her and smiled. She looked at me and did her best to hide her smile.

"Don't look at me like that," she said. "I'm still mad at you."

"What?... I just wanted to know where we're going."

"Sure... whatever," Rose replied. "I figured we should stop by the hospital then go to the morgue. I called the police station. The girls' parents should be picking them up from the station right now. They had quite the experience today, so I think it's best to give them some time before asking questions."

"It's going to be late before we get to the morgue."

"Don't worry, Mr. Black, I called. They're not quitting until after I get what I want," Rose grinned.

"Is that how it always is? No one can quit until you get what you want?"

Rose ogled me. "Don't start with me, Black."

After about ten minutes of driving, we pulled into the parking lot of the hospital. It took us four minutes to find a parking spot then make it into the hospital lobby, where we found two police officers on duty. Rose went up to the receptionist to get information for the rooms. This time, I decided to take the elevator up with her instead of the stairs. I didn't think there was much threatening us. Ireland, Bennett, and Bennett's two flunkies were all injured and in custody, and Smith, Felix, Williams, and Uchida were all dead. Yep, I felt pretty safe. The elevator dinged and the doors rolled open.

As we slid across the sleek hospital floor, the first room we approached had an officer outside the door. Rose flashed her badge, and then we walked freely into the room. Ireland was laid up with a cast wrapped around his leg. He was asleep and handcuffed to the bed. We decided to let him sleep.

"He probably wouldn't have much to say anyway," Rose whispered.

We strolled out of the room and hiked down the hall to another room guarded by yet another officer. Rose once again flashed her badge.

"Okay," the officer said. "He suffered a mild concussion. The doctor wants to keep him here overnight for observation. He should be free to go tomorrow... Well, not free, but you know what I mean."

"Thanks," Rose replied.

Rose and I stepped into the room. Bennett was lying in the bed with his eyes open. He looked to be in thought. He was wearing his nice slacks and his button-up white shirt, now dirty and unbuttoned at the top. He had medical bandages girted around his forehead. The metal handcuffs dinged against the alloy of the bed railing when he fidgeted upright at our entrance.

"Alex," Rose greeted.

"Special Agent Lee," Bennett responded. He sneered at me, and then he directed his attention to the wall in front of him at the foot of his bed. It was as if he was embarrassed about his involvement with Uchida's sick little operation. It made sense, considering he carried a badge that swore his allegiance to protecting the country.

"I have a few questions to ask you," Rose said.

"Save your breath. I know the drill. I'm not saying a thing without my lawyer," Bennett replied.

"Suit yourself, but you're going down hard for this. I'll make sure of it."

He continued to stare at the wall.

Rose and I stepped out of the room and walked towards the elevators.

"I knew he wasn't going to say anything," Rose said.

"Well, he said a mouthful by telling us he wouldn't speak without a lawyer," I replied.

"Yeah, the bastard is guilty and he knows he's going down. We have eyewitnesses, the pictures, and no telling what else we'll find when we look deep into his activities over the years with the Bureau."

A little under twenty minutes later, we were parking at the morgue. The door was locked, but Rose knocked briskly four times. After a few moments the sound of someone fiddling with the lock rang from the other side. Then it lightly swung open. Behind the door was a bearded middle-aged white man with salt-and-pepper hair.

"Agent Lee?" he said.

"Yes."

"Nice to meet you. Come on in." He shook our hands then led us to where the bodies were being kept. "Here they are," the man said simply.

There were four stretchers, and on them lay four bodies covered by thick white sheets.

"Their belongings are in evidence bags over on that table there," the man pointed across the bodies to the other side of the room. "Earlier the phones were ringing like crazy, one after the next. But anywho, I'll be down the hall if you need me."

"Thank you," Rose replied.

He smiled and then scooted out of the room.

Rose stuck her hand inside her pocket and came out with two black elastic nitrile gloves. She handed me one of the gloves, and we slid them on. She started with the body closest to us. I glanced over her shoulder as she lifted the first sheet. It was Smith. Although he had dark skin, his face had turned cold and pale.

"Okay, that's Craig Smith," Rose said.

She moved to the next body. Again I watched from over her shoulder. It was Williams. The third was Felix. When we stepped to the fourth and final stretcher in the room and Rose uncovered the face, I recognized him immediately as Uchida. She stared at his face in confusion.

"Uchida?" I said.

"No... Not— not really," she replied.

I immediately thought back to our meet in Rock Hill, where Davis asked me why I hadn't ID'ed Uchida from the pictures in the binder. Then I thought back to Sully Island at the hangar when Burns referred to Uchida as a boy, and how Uchida was running his mouth about what his father had taught him. Then it hit me. *I can't believe I missed it.*

"It's not Uchida. It's his son," I realized aloud.

CHAPTER
EIGHTEEN

"Yes, this is Uchida Junior," Rose confirmed.

She moved the sheet back over his face, then reached into her pocket and pulled out her phone. I watched as she swiped her thumb across the screen.

"See, here's Uchida Senior," she said as she swung the phone close to my face.

It was a snapshot of the picture Burns had taken. The picture showed Bennett and Uchida Senior on the beach near the airstrip in Sully Island. From their gestures you could tell they were talking. Behind the two of them stood the beach house, with two young white females hanging out nearby. The females' faces were a little difficult to make out, but I was sure I'd never seen them before. The two girls appeared to be smiling and enjoying themselves.

I nodded.

Rose put the phone back in her pocket. "So Uchida is still out there," she said.

"Yeah, it appears that way."

I walked over to the table of belongings with Rose following behind me. There were four bags. We examined the contents and found various paraphernalia; a couple of them had wallets, some with jewelry, badges, and a number of other insignificant things such as loose change, but one thing they all contained were cell phones. We checked three of them —the fourth was a little wet and wouldn't power on. I figured that was Williams' phone, which probably got wet during our scuffle and his demise. All three of the cell phones we checked had missed calls from the same Asheville number. One phone had only one missed call from the number, the second had three, and the last cell phone had seven.

"Who is in possession of Bennett's cell phone?" I asked.

"I think the local PD may still have it," Rose replied.

"I'm sure he has received calls from this same number. Uchida is scrambling."

"That's a good thing, right?"

"I'm not sure yet."

We thanked the gentleman at the morgue for his help, and then bounced. As we were walking to the car, Rose made a phone call, so I thought it'd be a good time to try Daniels again. I dialed his number but again got nothing but his voicemail. Rose was still speaking on her phone as we entered the car. After about another minute she hung up.

"That was the local PD," she told me. "They confirmed Bennett's cell phone had some missed calls from the same number."

Rose then dialed up Davis and told him that the body was Uchida Junior, not Senior, and asked if he could try to track down Uchida's current location. We pulled out of the morgue and onto the road.

"You hungry?" Rose asked.

"I could eat."

"Okay, I think I saw an all-night diner in town."

The ride to the diner was quiet. I was deep in my thoughts, but I could tell Rose was sharing her attention between the road and me. She didn't speak. I knew she wanted to know what was going on in my mind, but I guess she wanted to give me some time to work through my reflections myself. Once at the diner, we picked a booth and placed our orders.

"So are you going to tell me what's on your mind, Black?" Rose asked.

"Is it that obvious?" I asked. "I'm usually better at hiding it."

"Or maybe I just better understand you now," Rose smiled.

I smiled back. "Just haven't heard anything back from Daniels or Nicole."

"They're probably lying low. I'm sure we'll hear from them soon."

"I felt a little better about it when Uchida was dead in my mind, but now that I know he's still out there…"

"I have Davis looking into where Uchida is now, so we'll find him. I'm really thankful for all of your help, but I thought you'd be happy to rid yourself of this."

"Not yet—my work isn't finished."

Rose reached across the table and grabbed my hand. "You can't help yourself, can you?" she said.

We fixated on each other's faces for a long moment. Rose was really so beautiful. She wore the Asian and black mixture perfectly. Her skin was a smooth, beautiful dark olive tone. Her straight, slightly curly black hair was alluring and her smile was absolutely breathtaking. Our moment was broken when the waitress brought us our food. We sat and ate, and then we talked and laughed for a while. It had been some time since I'd had such a good time. It was great—even amazing—and it helped to take our minds off of all the calamity. Before I knew it, hours had passed and we were in the early morning of the next day.

"Whoa, we better get out of here," Rose said.

"Yeah you're right," I replied.

We'd already paid for our food, so we walked out of the

diner. My phone rang in my pocket and I stopped to remove it. Rose continued on a few steps ahead before turning back in my direction. Seeing that it was Daniels' number on the screen, I hit the answer button and raised the phone to my ear.

"Hello," I answered.

The line hissed quietly for a brief moment. Then a voice eased on the line, a mature, confident, poised voice. But it wasn't Daniels'.

"Hello, Mr. Black," the voice said. I knew who it was. One of the scenarios I'd played out in my head was beginning to transpire.

"Don't act like you know me, you piece of crap!" I replied bitterly.

Rose stepped closer towards me, confused, wanting to know who was on the other side of the phone.

"Where is he, Uchida? Where's Daniels?" I continued.

Rose's eyes lit up. I raised my hand between us, to signal for her to remain silent.

"He's here with us and he's unharmed. He'll remain that way if you do exactly what I tell you. Do you understand, Mr. Black?"

"The only thing I understand is you're going down and you know it. Why else would you be calling me?" I replied.

"I read some of your file, Mr. Black. The parts that weren't redacted were pretty impressive. You and I are similar in a lot of ways. I was even thinking of hiring you at one point."

"You and me alike... Just for saying that I'll make especially sure I kick your teeth in when I see you."

"I said similar, not just alike. See, you seem to have a moral compass that I do not have. Let me show you what I mean. Bring her here." The last sentence he said to someone near him.

I heard a woman's voice in the background screaming. It

was a voice I recognized. *Nicole.* I closed my eyes and hung my head.

"Mrs. Burns, would you like to talk to Mr. Black?" Uchida said. "Oh... you're not in the talking mood. You must be stressed. There are some things that I and the boys can do to loosen you up."

"Okay, okay, what do you want, you bastard?" I said quietly.

"I thought that might help get your attention. Now that we have an understanding—have you been in contact with Detective Burns?"

"Yes, I have, I was able to locate and free him. Nice house and plane, by the way."

"Well, Detective Burns may be in the possession of something that's of interest to my organization and clients. You'll bring it to me."

"What makes you think he'd give it to me?"

"Mr. Black. My patience is running thin. Either you find it or Detective Daniels here dies. Then I'll find Detective Burns and kill him too. But I won't stop there. I'll let the boys have a little fun with Mrs. Burns and then that beautiful FBI agent... Lee, is it? She will be a fun one. Then I'll find Burns' daughter and take the three of them on the *Carolina Dance* to fetch a nice penny. Do you get the picture, Mr. Black?"

As I was listening to Uchida, all I could think is, *I'm talking to a dead man.* I hadn't blown my top since the beginning of the whole mess, which was shocking. And I technically hadn't killed anyone either, which was even more shocking to me. But I knew just as I was standing there holding the phone that Uchida was finished. By mentioning Rose, he pushed my motivation beyond a promise I had made to a stranger. He had made it personal. But I had to play along.

"Yeah, I get it."

"Good, let me give you the details." And he gave me an Asheville address.

"To get all of this and reach you it'll take me at least eight hours," I said.

"That's too long," Uchida replied.

"What do you expect? If you don't like the timetable why don't you get one of your lackeys to do it? Smith, Evans, Ireland, Williams, Bennett, or your son. Yeah, have Junior, your own flesh and blood, do it."

The line went quiet for a moment. I could tell Uchida knew something was going on. He knew something had happened to little Uchida Junior, but he had to remain poised and in control.

"You have exactly five hours to get me what I asked for. If you don't, I'll do exactly as I said I would!" he gritted.

The call then immediately dropped.

I pulled the phone from my ear then dropped it in my pocket. Rose glared at me with suspense.

"So... Wh— who was that?" she asked.

I paced towards the car. "C'mon, I'll tell you on the way back."

During the first few minutes of the car ride, I shared all the details of the call with her.

"So Uchida has both Daniels and Nicole?" she asked.

"Yes, in Asheville," I responded.

"I'm going to call Davis."

Rose had one hand on the steering wheel and used her other hand to thumb her phone before raising it to her ear. "Hey, you awake?" she asked through the phone. "Well, nap time is over. Are you alone?... Okay, good. Black just received a call from Uchida. He has Daniels and Nicole hostage. ...Yes I know... Well, he called from Daniels' number. He gave Black an Asheville address and wants Burns' envelope delivered to him in less than five hours. ...Wait, let me ask. Black, what was the address?"

I gave her the address Uchida had given me.

She repeated the address to Davis. "...Right, from the

sound of it he doesn't know we've already reviewed the evidence... That I'm not sure of."

I listened to the conversation. We didn't have much time to follow procedure and to be diplomatic, so I intervened.

"Rose, ask Davis if Hicks is still around," I said.

"Okay," she said to me. Then she spoke into the phone, "Is Hicks still around the base?" she asked. "...Okay, he's there, Black."

"Ask if he can give me a ride to Asheville," I said.

Rose moved the phone away from her mouth. "If need be, I can take you, Black," she said.

"Not faster than a chopper," I replied.

Rose smiled then moved the phone closer to her lips. "See if Hicks can loan us a helicopter and a pilot if needed... Okay, we'll be there shortly," she said into the phone.

She ended the call, glanced over at me, and then sighed before tightening her grip on the steering wheel and directing her focus towards the road. Back at the Coast Guard base, Davis was waiting for us at the gate. On our way to the same bunk room we used earlier, we passed by the lounge area where Burns and Madeline were still sound asleep on the couch. In the bunk room there was a small stack of documents laid out on the sofa. Davis walked over to the sofa and picked up the stack.

"The address you gave me is for Uchida's home in Asheville," he said. "I was looking at some of the pictures and floor plans we'd gathered from the house earlier in our investigation into him for his white-collar crime."

Davis passed the pictures and floor plans to Rose, and I viewed them over her shoulder. The house was large, maybe eight bedrooms. It sat by itself at the top of a hill and had no gate or fence surrounding it. Rose handed the stack to me. I shuffled through the floor plan.

"I was thinking we should call the local PD," Davis said. "They can reach the house much faster than we can."

I shook my head. "I don't think we want to sound the alarm until we know both Nicole and Daniels are safe."

Both Rose and Davis nodded.

I committed the floor plans to memory and handed the documents over to Davis. "Does Uchida have any sentries that you know of? I'd imagine he does because of how big the house is."

"Yeah, I believe we noticed three during one of our earlier stakeouts on this place," Davis answered. "Two guards in the front and one in the back."

Hicks walked into the room. "Hey, I have something for you guys. Follow me," he said.

We trailed behind Hicks down the hall. Hicks used his key card at a door, which beeped then clicked open. We entered a room for monitoring and surveillance. It reminded me of a small command center: There were a few monitors set up showing video from various cameras around the base, and there were some radar and sonar systems. The room was dimly lit and had a few officers monitoring the equipment. At the center of the room was a large square table. We followed Hicks over to it.

On the table, spread open, was a satellite image of the area surrounding Uchida's home in Asheville—I recognized the house immediately by its shape. Next to the printed image were a couple of markers.

"Will this do?" Hicks asked Davis.

"Yeah this should work," Davis responded.

Rose and Davis surveyed the printed image.

"Hicks, how long will it take to get to this area by helicopter?" I asked.

"Maybe an hour, hour fifteen minutes."

I took one of the markers, leaned over the table, and circled Uchida's house. "This is the house," I said. "We just need to find a place to land that's close by, but not too close."

"What's that behind the house?" Rose pointed.

"Looks like a helipad," Hicks said. "We can land there."

I pulled myself up straight from over the table. "That'd be a good place to land in case of an emergency," I said. "But there are two hostages and probably around eight enemy combatants. We'll need a place to come in unnoticed."

I pointed to an area west of the house. It looked open, clear, and flat. It was far enough not to be spotted but close enough to travel to the house by foot. "If you can get me here I can hike the rest of the way to the house. Once I get in and rescue Nicole and Daniels then we can call in the reinforcements," I stated.

Rose took a step back, folding her arms. "Wait, you think you're going in there alone?" she said.

"Yeah, Black, that's a bit cocky," Davis followed.

"I'm confident I can handle the situation myself," I said.

"Look, Black, I read your file, I believe in you too, but for the sake of Daniels and Mrs. Burns, I think someone should go with you," Rose said.

Although I was sure I could handle the situation myself, it would be better to have backup, especially in a hostage situation. I really didn't want Rose around Uchida after the remarks he had made. I didn't want her to see who I'd become if he made another threat, let alone if she got hurt.

"Okay, sure," I said.

"I can lend you two additional men for support," Hicks said.

"That'll help," Rose responded.

"And we can have the local PD ready to move in. We just need a plan now," Davis added.

"Hey, Davis, hand me those floor plans," I said.

Davis poked the documents in my direction. I grabbed the documents and placed them on the table next to the satellite image to study them. Hicks started towards the door.

"I'll go get the two guys and the pilot so they can be included in the brief," Hicks said.

"Okay, I need to get some equipment out of the car," Davis said.

"Wait, Ben, I need to grab some stuff too. Plus, I have the key," Rose said.

My attention was fixed on the table. I faintly heard the three of them scramble out of the room and the door smack shut behind them as I deliberated the information in front of me. The visual chess board was positioned in my mind. It felt like I was back at my old job on the government payroll. I considered the adversary, I considered my allies, and I considered the apprehended. I analyzed where in the house Nicole and Daniels would most likely be held.

Minutes passed before the beep and click of the door permeated through the room. I could hear multiple footsteps approaching me and then surrounding the table. At that moment it hit me. I had a plan—a plan A, B, and C, as a matter of fact. I looked up from the table. Rose and Davis were carrying some gear, including a couple MP10 rifles and vests with "FBI" printed across the front. Hicks stood next to three gentlemen in green combat camouflage fatigues. They were all lieutenants, according to the "Lt." showing on their name tags.

"Hicks, you guys have comms, right?" I asked.

"Affirmative, plenty of 'em," Hicks answered.

I smiled. "I have a plan."

CHAPTER
NINETEEN

I explained the plan I had, which everyone agreed was the best course of action under the circumstances.

"Sounds like a plan. Let's do it," Hicks approved.

One of the three guys dressed in uniform nodded. "Sir, we'll secure the comms, gear up, and make sure the chopper is ready."

The three left the room. I checked the time on my phone; it was a little after an hour since Uchida had called.

"We'd better gear up too," Rose said. "Here, Black."

She handed me a Kevlar vest, which didn't have "FBI" written on it. It was flexible and lightweight. I could wear it under my shirt and coat with no problem.

"Thanks," I said. "Do you guys have any spare firearms?"

Rose fumbled around with the gear she was carrying. Clipped to the FBI bulletproof vest she held was a holstered Glock 22. She passed it to me, holster and all.

"Sorry, we don't have any spare rifles," she said.

"Oh, this should be more than enough."

I reached behind my back and clipped the gun to my belt, centered at my lower back. Rose, Davis, and I then marched out of the room, found the nearest restrooms, and geared up. I went into a stall in the men's restroom and put the Kevlar on under my shirt and coat. Davis was in the restroom with me. I could hear the Velcro straps from his vest scratching apart then crunching together. I pulled the Glock from the holster, inspected it, and placed it back into the holster. I then lifted one foot at a time on the toilet seat to tighten the straps of my knife holsters around my ankles, and I stepped outside of the stall. Davis was near the sink prepping his rifle. His blazer was off and the FBI vest was strapped over his white long-sleeved button-up shirt. I nodded at him as I walked out of the restroom. He nodded back.

I strolled back to the door of the command center, which was locked. I didn't have a card, so I just waited. Davis came down the hall with Rose behind him, both geared up with their vest, rifles, and side arms. After a brief moment, two of the three lieutenants from earlier made their way to us, dressed as before but toting rifles and wearing helmets to match. One of them swiped his card and cracked the door open while another handed Rose, Davis, and me comm units, which consisted of a small walkie-talkie, a throat mic, and an ear piece. It had a simple push-to-talk setup and it was light-weight and great for covert operations. The five of us fell into the operation center, where Hicks was waiting for us around the table. We all set up our comm equipment and confirmed we could communicate with one another. Not long after, the third lieutenant of the group, who was also the pilot, entered. He marched over to us then faced Hicks.

"The chopper is ready, sir," he declared.

"Thanks, lieutenant," Hicks responded.

The pilot then left the room. The room was overflowing with the sounds of ruffled gear and radio buzz.

"Everyone ready to get topside?" Hicks asked.

There were a lot of head nods around the table in response. Ten minutes later, we were all flying over Charleston—with the exception of Hicks, who stayed back at the base. Inside the helicopter cockpit were the pilot and one of the other lieutenants. In the cabin sat Rose, Davis, the third Coast Guard lieutenant, and me. Everyone sat quietly while wearing the helicopter headphones. I looked through the window, out into the clear, starry sky of early morning. It was still and peaceful outside, just as it was inside the cabin, minus the roar from the helicopter's main rotor. Everyone was calm. This wasn't any of our first rodeos, and there was very little tension.

About halfway through the flight, the lieutenant sitting in the cabin with Rose, Davis, and me reached inside a compartment under the seats. He handed both Rose and Davis flashlights. Twenty-five or thirty minutes later we were soaring above Asheville and soon were floating over Uchida's house from far above. As known, the house was on the top of a small hill. The hill was not very steep; it would be easy to drive or even walk up to the house. Surrounding the house was forest blotted with a number of open fields that circled maybe a half mile radius around the house. We traveled west of the house. We were about a quarter of a mile away from the house before we began to descend close to a flat, open field.

The pilot spoke into the headphones we were wearing. "We're here," he announced.

The Coast Guardsman in the cabin with us stood and opened the helicopter's side cabin door. "Let's go!" he yelled against the rushing sound created by the chopper.

I removed my headphones and stepped towards the cabin door, looking out. The helicopter was on the ground, and I could see a wind cyclone made of dirt, grass, sticks, and twigs swirling around us. Other than that, everything looked quiet and tranquil. I hopped out onto the springy grass, and right away the reflexes I had developed by habit over the years kicked in. I immediately moved a couple yards away from the helicopter, dropped to one knee, pulled out the Glock in shooting position, and quickly surveyed the area. I hit the push-to-talk button on my comms.

"The ground is clear," I said through the comms.

"Roger that," the lieutenant replied.

The comms were reading loud and clear; it felt like he was right next to me speaking in my ear. Seconds later, Rose and Davis exited the helicopter. They touched ground and, against the cyclone power of the helicopter, they dragged themselves towards me. We waved the helicopter off then it ascended.

"We'll head a little further west," the lieutenant riding shotgun in the cockpit buzzed into the comms. "But we'll be here for air support and ground support if needed. Watch your six out there."

"Copy that," I replied.

The chopper continued west and disappeared into the darkness of the sky. Rose, Davis, and I journeyed east towards Uchida's house. We marched across the field and through the woods, navigating the slight incline the entire time. It was dark, and although I could see just fine, I followed slightly behind Rose and Davis since they had the flashlights. It was a matter of minutes before the house was in sight.

We ducked behind some bushes where the ground was at a lower elevation than the foundations of the house. The bushes plus the slope of the ground provided us both stealth cover and cover from enemy fire, if we ended up needing it. Rose and Davis cut off their flashlights. We were about twenty-five yards away from the front corner of the west side of the house. I charily bellied up the slope and peeped over the bushes. I could see the front of the house and noted that the grounds were well kept and the house had a few shrubs scattered along its walls. There were two guards patrolling. One was closer to the side of the house where we were hidden and the other was across the yard near the east side of the house. It was hard to make out because of the darkness, but the guard closer to us appeared to be wearing a suit and carrying some type of submachine gun, which was strapped over his shoulder. Towards the back of the house a vehicle was parked—either a dark-colored van or SUV. There was a guard trekking from behind the back of the house past the dark vehicle and along the west side wall towards the front of the building. Rose and Davis crawled up to where I was.

"Looks like there are only three of them," Davis whispered.

"That's what we planned for," Rose said quietly. "We can't see the east side of the house, plus it's dark. I hope there isn't another guard on the far side."

As Rose and Davis were speaking, I carefully observed the patterns of the three guards. I noticed their walking route and tried to time it the best I could in my mind. I noticed certain behaviors they displayed, like where they would stop in their route before turning around, in which directions they would look, when they would take their hands off their guns and stretch... The basic things a human would do by habit without realizing it. I was waiting for an opportunity. It was a little under two hours from the time Uchida was expecting to see me, so we still had the element of time and surprise to our advantage, but I preferred to move quickly.

I continued to watch, and then it happened—an opportunity opened. I raced from behind the bushes up to the house. I was silent but quick. I mean, lightning quick. It felt like I'd taken only two steps before I was on the guard who was pacing towards the back of the house. He was in front of the black vehicle, which turned out to be a van. I didn't give the van too much attention because I had only one objective in mind at that moment. It all happened so fast. My training and muscle memory took over: I hit the guard with the same move I'd used on Ireland at the Epic Center, simultaneously smashing my elbow and thrusting the valley of my hand against his neck. As he fell back I caught him, removed the submachine gun strapped over his shoulder, and then allowed him to flatten backwards to the ground. I seized the submachine gun, which was a MP5K with a shoulder stock, and laid it behind a shrub near the wall of the house. Then I dashed along the wall to the front of the house. The second guard was at the corner, just as I had planned. I had timed it flawlessly.

I saw the front of his gun before I saw him. I grabbed the hand he was holding the gun with and immediately twisted it so he couldn't pull the trigger. I clutched the back of his neck with my other hand and swung him around in front of me, slamming him head first into the side wall. The collision put him sound to sleep.

I removed the MP5K from his collapsed body, threw the strap over my shoulder, and then pointed the barrel towards the back of the house. My gaze was in perfect alignment with the rear and front sights of the gun. I then hurried towards the rear of the house. Everything had happened in a matter of seconds; I confirmed this by briefly glancing back in the direction of Rose and Davis, who had just stepped from behind the bushes where we had been hiding. I kept my aim with the gun as I slipped between the van and the wall of the house towards the back. The night made my vision a bit dull. I was able to see the helipad to my left and the back wall of the house was to my right. There was some light coming from the house, but none coming from the outside rooms. Before I knew it, I was already at the rear east corner of the house. I took cover behind the wall and peeked around the corner.

I saw the third perimeter guard making his way towards me but stopping just before he got to the back of the house. By the shuffle of his feet I knew he was turning around, which was my opportunity. I removed the strap of the gun from over my shoulder and cradled the gun in both hands as I cut around the corner. I shoved the shoulder stock of the gun into the back of the guard's skull, and his body dropped directly over his feet as he fell into a nap. I strapped the gun back over my shoulder, took his gun and hid it behind some shrubs near the house, then carried him on my back to the west side of the house.

As I made my way around the van I heard the rustling of a gun being aimed at me.

"Geez... Black, I could've shot you," Rose whispered. "What was that?"

I continued past the van and laid the third guard next to the first one whom I had knocked out. "He was the last one on the perimeter," I replied.

Davis was zip-tying the hands and feet of the guard whose head I rammed into the wall. He looked over at me. "That wasn't part of the plan, Black," he whispered.

Rose walked around me, to the side of me where Davis was. "No kidding. Next time you do something like that, fill us in first. We're following your plan, remember," she whispered.

"Sometimes I have to improvise," I said. "Do you have any more zip ties?"

We tied the hands and feet of the guards and, since the three of them were all wearing neck ties, we used those to gag them. None of the guards were carrying any other weapons, identification, keys... nada.

"Now what?" Davis asked.

I looked back towards the van. "We can put them in the back of this van," I suggested.

Since the perimeter guards were taken out, I had a chance to really pause and look at the van up close. I was sure it was the same van that Evans had been driving.

"Okay, I guess we better move them then," Davis said.

Just as Davis finished speaking, a noise clanked from the van. The noise was almost quiet enough to be nothing, but loud enough to get our attention. There was no one in the front driver or passenger seat, so we knew the noise had to come from the back. I aimed the MP5K at the van, and Rose and Davis followed suit with their FBI-issued rifles. Together we eased around to the back of the van. It had dual cabin doors, with each swinging outward on either side. I signaled for Rose and Davis to open the doors. Rose was to my left and Davis my right. They both clutched the door handle of each of their respective doors. I held up three fingers, then two, then only one, and then grasped the front stock of the MP5K. Rose and Davis tugged against the doors and they flapped open. Inside the van was dark. The two sides of the interior were lined with benches. On the bed of the cabin rested two flat tires. From the darkness behind them, a grunt reached our ears. I stepped up and looked closer. It was Daniels, tied up on the cabin floor towards the front. His shirt was dingy and ripped. There were a few minor bruises and cuts spotted over his face, neck, and chest.

I hopped inside the van. "It's Daniels," I whispered back to Rose and Davis.

I took one of my knives and cut his restraints. He was a little out of it but was coherent and able to move. I helped him out of the van.

He walked gingerly and looked at me with a tired gaze. "Man, am I happy to see you, Black," he sighed.

"Hi Pete... how are you holding up?" Rose asked.

"I'm fine, but we have to get Nicole, she's in the house... It's my fault. I told them where she was. They still have Frank and Madeline. I heard them talking about some girls in Charleston too..."

"Hey, hey, calm down," I said. "Can you tell us where Nicole is at in the house?"

"I can show you exactly where she's at," he replied.

I watched Daniels favor his left leg. The injury appeared very minor, but it would only take one mistake. One bad move and everything could go tumbling down.

"I don't think that's a good idea," I said. "I just need you to tell me where she's at."

"Yeah, you look hurt," Rose added.

"It's just a scratch. I'll be fine."

"We should get going," Davis said.

Daniels nodded. "She's on the east side of the house, second floor, back corner room. Be careful, there are five of them inside," he said.

I jogged over to the hedges where I had thrown the first guard's MP5K, removed the gun from the shrubs, then dashed back over and handed the gun to Daniels. As I did that, Davis radioed back to the Coast Guard helicopter over the comms letting them know the situation and plan had changed.

"Okay, you guys take Daniels somewhere safe. I'm going in to get Nicole," I said.

"By yourself?" Davis asked.

"No way, Black," Rose followed up. "I'm going with you. Remember, you're a civilian."

I didn't bother arguing with her, since I could see her mind was made up.

"I'll take Daniels over to where we were hiding earlier," Davis said.

"We'll keep you updated over the comms," Rose replied.

Davis and Daniels walked away across the well-groomed grassy field towards the slope behind the lush green bushes. There was a door on the side wall near where the van was parked. I dashed over to it, removed the lock pick tool, dropped to one knee, and then went to work on it. Rose was behind me on lookout.

"You know I can do this myself?" I said.

"Black, just shut up and get the door open. We don't have a lot of time."

The truth was I cared about her and didn't want to see anything happen to her. I reminded myself that Special Agent Lee was no pushover and, although I knew I could handle the situation myself, it didn't hurt to have some help. I knew that she could handle herself just fine. The door clicked unlocked. I signaled to Rose then carefully turned the knob and pushed the door inward with the submachine gun aimed in front of me. The door quietly swayed open.

I stepped in first, Rose tailing me. We were in the kitchen. The lights were off. Straight ahead of us we could see into a sitting room which led out the back door to the helipad. The room was dim with small streaks of light beaming into it. I could hear Rose's voice over the comms.

"We're in," she whispered.

We turned to our right where the kitchen opened into a dining room. There was a large table in the middle of the room which could probably seat fifteen or sixteen people. We made a left then crouched into the living area, which was showered with light from an expensive chandelier hanging from the second floor ceiling high above. From the living room there was access to a connecting hallway and a staircase leading up to the second floor. To our right was the foyer area and front door and to our left, the living room opened into the sitting room we'd seen from the kitchen. Upstairs consisted of two hallway corridors connected by two walkways. Before heading upstairs, Rose and I checked down the hall east of the living room. There were no visuals but we could hear faint chatter coming from down the hall near the front of the house. The two of us vigilantly crept upstairs.

From upstairs we could look over the walkway and see the sitting room below on one side and the living room below on the other. Up here, all was quiet. I knelt and looked around, inspecting the entire floor from my central vantage point. It was clear. We eased to the door of the bedroom located at the back east corner of the house. Rose covered the hallway with her rifle while I cautiously rotated the door handle. It was unlocked. I cracked the door then very gently pushed to open it.

I checked the room with the MP5K as my guide. It was

quiet. I gestured for Rose's attention. She directed her aim towards the bedroom door. I softly flung the door open, just enough so Rose and I could enter. I zipped in and Rose scooted in behind me. The room was unlit with only stripes of moonlight cutting through from a window. I could see an empty bed but nothing else.

I hope Daniels didn't give us bad intel.

Rose softly closed the door. Then the room wasn't as quiet: There was a shadow moving in the blackness behind her. Rose saw me gape and throw my hand past her—she turned around to see a small lamp stand hovering inches from her face. Buffered between her face and the lamp stand was my hand. Rose stumbled backwards, aiming her gun in the direction of the shadow. I let the MP5K strapped over my shoulder drape down my side. With my free hand I halted Rose.

"Wait, wait, wait…" I whispered to the shadow. "We're here to help."

Nicole stepped into a ribbon of moonlight.

"Mr. Black," she whimpered.

"Oh… Mrs. Burns," Rose relaxed.

I grabbed the lamp stand from Nicole and softly rested it on the floor.

"Did they hurt you?" I asked.

Nicole shook her head in the negative.

"Good, we're gonna get you out of here," I said.

CHAPTER
TWENTY

I cracked the room door open and peeked outside. It was clear, at least from my vantage point. I looked back to Rose and Nicole.

"Ready?" I asked.

Rose nodded.

"Wait," Nicole whispered. She removed the Glock that was holstered to the back of my belt. She ejected the magazine, inspected it, and reinserted it back into the gun.

"Now I'm ready," Nicole nodded.

"You know how to use that?" I asked.

"My father's a colonel in the military and my husband's a cop, remember?"

I smiled then looked outside the room once again.

"Let's go," I said.

As we exited the room, I scanned across the second floor. It was clear. From over the railing of the walkway I checked the first floor but saw no activity. I heard Rose's voice over my shoulder.

"We have Nicole. We're heading out now," she said over the comms.

Rose and Nicole started down the stairs, Rose first. I

watched from the second floor walkway as the two made their way down the stairs and into the living room. They started for the dining room to their right, taking the same path Rose and I had used upon entering. Everything seemed to be going well... until it went sideways, fast.

I heard the two ladies gasp. I saw Rose raise her rifle towards the foyer near the front of the house. At the same time, Nicole began to jog towards the dining room. I side-stepped to my right to see whom Rose was targeting. Peering down to the first floor, I saw Evans and Uchida emerging from the hallway entrance on the left, near the foyer area. I rested the machine gun on top of the walkway rail to get a better aim on the two men. They were talking, Evans toting a slick gleaming silver pistol in his right hand and his left hand wrapped in bandages from the knife I had stuck in it roughly two days before. Uchida was carrying some type of sawed-off double-barrel shotgun. The two were not holding their weapons for use in that moment; rather, they seemed to be more of a precaution.

But then Evans saw Rose with her rifle targeted on him and froze. Uchida didn't appear to see Rose yet—his attention was focused on Nicole, who was racing for the dining room. Uchida began to stride towards her. All of it happened fast, but time itself froze when Rose uttered the words,

"FBI! Drop your weapons!"

I inhaled a deep breath. Everyone began to move in slow motion, including myself. My mind was moving rapidly, but my body was suspended in a tardy state. Rose had her rifle on Evans and he had his hands down to his side. His face started to slowly alter, tension wrinkling across it. Nicole was steps away from the entrance to the dining room. Uchida sprang in her direction. He slid into a shooting position, leaning forward, stretching, and raising the arm he was carrying the shotgun in. My aim was currently on Evans, who was lifting his gun up towards Rose. He didn't stand a chance. Rose had the MP10 pointed directly at his chest. Before Evans could lift his gun above his waist, Rose fired off two rounds. I knew Evans was done for, and I'd already begun to change my aim towards Uchida.

He lifted the shotgun with his right hand, and the momentum from his motion threw his left hand behind him at the same time, exposing his back widely to my aim. Nicole was nearing the dining room entrance and Uchida was heaving the sawed-off upwards. He looked like he was raising a heavy object from over a ledge with only one arm. I was struggling against my suspended state, trying to get a dead aim on him. I knew that with that weapon, he didn't have to be accurate with his aim. The buckshot spread could hit his target even if he was half a foot off the mark. I locked in on the back of his right shoulder. He was still lifting the gun, but it was aimed about forty-five degrees downward towards the floor. Another twenty or twenty-five degrees upward, and the buckshot spread would have hit Nicole. I was moving my aim towards his head, but felt I wouldn't find the shot in time. So I settled for the back of his right shoulder.

I squeezed the trigger and two rounds clapped from the MP5K. I heard a mixture of sounds. I could hear the blast from the gun slowly ringing, the buzz from the comm line opening, Rose exhaling, the sound of Evan's body dropping to the floor, Nicole screaming, and Uchida grunting. He was able to lift the shotgun another twelve or fifteen degrees before the first bullet penetrated near the rotator cuff of his right shoulder. The second bullet hit closer to his trapezius muscle. The force sent him spinning to his left towards the front door. The shotgun fired and the buckshot shattered into the floor just a few feet shy of the door, while the buckshot and fragments from the floor erupted into the air. Shrapnel flew back towards Uchida, hitting him, twisting him back towards his right.

My slow-motion suspension broke after I blew a deep exhale, so deep that I felt the knot of air coming undone from within my chest as I released it. Everyone began to move at normal speed again.

Davis crackled onto the comms. "What's going on in there?"

Nicole disappeared into the dining room. Uchida dropped the shotgun just before crashing backwards onto the floor. Evans' lifeless body lay stretched out on the floor. Rose looked back up at me.

"Go!" I yelled to her.

She raced towards the dining room. I didn't bother taking the stairs down—I leaped over the railings of the walkway and landed in the living room on bended knees. The very moment I stood straight, my body wanted to sprint towards the dining room. But I couldn't. My mind prohibited me, because I saw something.

From the corner of my eye I caught a glimpse of a white streak approaching my face very rapidly. I leaned back and my hands elevated in the air as a result. I was holding the gun with both hands, so the gun was in the position where my head was just a microsecond before. The white streak smacked the machine gun out of my hands and sent it clanging to the floor, then skidding into the dining room. The white streak was a right leg, covered by white pants, and a right foot wearing a white Adidas shoe. I knew it was one of the Kwon twins. He hooked his leg back towards me, targeting my head with the back of his heel. He was fast and agile—but not fast enough. I folded into the kick and pushed his leg away. He followed up with a Dol Gae Chagi, or tornado kick, with the same leg. I moved into his kick to minimize its power, and then lightly hooked his leg under my arm, and, using the spinning momentum from his kick, I landed a palm strike into his chest. The force from those combined elements tossed him over a couch and sent him smashing into the staircase.

I looked to the floor and saw a shadow spreading under me. I looked up in time to see the other twin plunging down towards me from the walkway on the second floor. He descended towards me forming an E Dan Yop Chagi—a flying side kick. I swiftly jumped backwards, raising both of my forearms together in the form of a cross to absorb the weight of his kick. It was enough to shuffle me back until I was just barely in the dining room. I quickly looked to my left, catching sight of Rose as she exited the kitchen door, the same one we had used to enter the house.

The second twin stood in front of me in the living room just a couple feet short of the dining room entrance. He grinned, proud that his attack had made contact. I studied his face for a second and noticed he had a small scar just above his right eye. Close to his forehead. I remembered what Rose said concerning the twins' distinguishing scars.

So, Leonard, huh... grin while you can, punk, there's a beat-down coming your way. Shall we dance?

I relaxed into my fighting stance. I saw the first twin, Leo, toppling over the stairs, struggling to find his legs under him. Leonard noticed my short moment of distraction and twisted backwards into a stance, then launched at me with a spinning back kick. It was predictable, being a move I had practiced many times before. I was able to stop him before he picked up momentum by delivering a straight front kick of my own to his kicking leg. That sent his leg swinging back in the opposite direction. The rest of his body swung with his leg, turning a complete three-sixty turn. He then hurdled from the dining room entrance towards me with a Superman punch. I calmly waited until I felt he was sure that he would land the punch, then slipped to the outside under his punch and connected with his chin using an uppercut palm strike. His head shot backwards, and his body followed. His hands scuffled to grip the wall as he fell back and tumbled into the living room. Leo rushed towards me, dodging his brother's rolling body. I jumped on top of the large dining room table.

Rose's voice panted on the comms. "I have Nicole. Black is still in the house."

At that point I removed the ear piece from my ear to avoid the distraction. Leo picked that moment to vault towards me with two kicks. He was high in the air, high enough to kick with his right leg then his left leg and land on top of the dining room table with me. I parried both kicks. He threw a left roundhouse kick at me, which I blocked; then he followed up with an axe kick, which I fleeted under before pivoting behind him. Before he realized, I had my forearm under the back of his ribcage and was using my other hand to push my forearm further into his ribcage. It was a rapid explosive push, but I delivered it smoothly. The force knocked against his ribcage then thrust him along the length of the table. He dove forward and slid nearly to the end of the table on the opposite side of the kitchen.

He then jumped to his feet, anger and frustration all over his face. He clasped his teeth. "Argh!" he gritted.

He began to pitch punches and kicks at me while I blocked and dodged them all. We were dancing around on top of the table. Leonard was back on his feet and rejoined the fight with a flying side kick onto the table. He missed. I was parrying and blocking both their attacks for a few seconds before I saw an opening. I hit both of them at the same time, for the first time, with closed fists, and they soared off the table to smack against the floor near the kitchen. I hopped down from the table to make my way through the kitchen and out the door.

But I had a problem. A really big problem. The giant Okamoto met me as soon as my feet touched the floor. He clenched my shoulder in his hands and blitzed forward, charging me backwards. We were gliding across the dining room then I felt something collide against my back. Broken wood was exposed and water spewed everywhere as drywall dust particles whisked in the air. There was a wrecked sink with water sprouting from it next to me, a massive hole in the wall where I could see into the dining room, and I was pressed between a wall and a toilet stool. My arms erupted upward then outward, breaking the grip Okamoto hand on my shoulders. Next I delivered a barrage of elbows to his head. The sound of my drenched coat squeaked against his equally drenched head. He closed his hands around my neck. I used my fists as hammers and pounded on his arms in a battle to get free. Then I realized something: I was trying too hard resisting. Okamoto's grip around my neck wasn't very tight. His hands were wet and my neck was soaked from the gush of water that was hitting the top of my head then streaming down my face and neck. I relaxed into a deep stance and grabbed his hands near the thumbs, then slowly peeled his hands away from my neck. He began to grunt while I started to whoop in effort. I pulled his hands from my neck then quickly formed a spear shape with both my hands, thrusting it into his throat. He immediately palmed his neck to soothe the pain. I rotated to my right, snatched the toilet lid from off the toilet, and bashed it square with his head. He wavered backwards and his newsboy cap fell off. I then thrust my elbow into his gut. He tottered backwards through the hole into the dining room.

Rage began to boil inside of me. I flew at him with a sideways two-legged drop kick, the type of kick you see wrestlers do. The kick united with his chest and slammed him into the end of the dining room table. The power from the impact drove the table back towards the kitchen. The table nearly crashed into the twins, but they saw it coming, leaped above it, and dashed across it towards me. I was struggling with my anger, contesting against it, not wanting it to blaze outward.

Calm down, Black, you can finish this without exploding.

I smothered the fury enough to focus on the fight, but I was still mad. The twins simultaneously loped over Okamoto, who was bent to one knee resting up against the end of the table, and sailed through the air towards me. Leo kicked at me and Leonard was just leaping in my direction. I knew if Leo's kick landed correctly, it would send me back into the bathroom. I caught his foot and bent my upper body inward to minimize the impact. It worked flawlessly. I yanked his leg towards me, and he fell to the floor. I then hooked his leg under my arm and twisted until I heard a pop.

He screamed.

Leonard rushed me but I repelled him with a front heel kick. Then with the same leg, I stamped Leo's skull, putting him in a snooze.

Leonard looked down at his brother's prostrate body then glared at me.

I threw Leo's inanimate leg down, then glared back at Leonard without a single care in the world.

"Grrr!" he huffed.

He slung a roundhouse kick at me. I threw it back at him with my forearm. He immediately pursued with a turning kick. I slid into the kick, hooking his leg under my arm, then I axed my elbow downward just above his knee. A crack resounded from his leg, followed by an "Oww!" from his mouth. I used the same elbow to strike the side of his face. Next I kneed him in the stomach and bashed the side of his face again with a back fist. All my attacks were fast and fluent, and my movements flowed as one smooth motion. Leonard hit the dining room floor and joined his brother Leo in a nap.

The twins lay wasted in front of me. The two were no longer a threat to me, but the indignation that raged inside of me wanted more. I wanted to kick and stomp their feeble, mangled bodies until I was sure they wouldn't be a problem for anyone ever again. I was falling into the old familiar raging trance. A dense somber film began to shutter my vision while the weight of my breathing became heavier. I shook my head, trying hard to break the trance.

I jolted my head again from side to side. My chaotic stupor broke. My vision returned to normal, my breathing regulated. A wave of calm gradually shrouded me. I focused on the sound of my breath going in and out of my lungs. I heard the splashing water pouring onto the dining room floor from the hole in the wall. I heard the sound of the Coast Guard helicopter approaching the house and the sound of ruffling from the giant surging to his feet.

With poise I faced Okamoto. His eyes were wide open, his eyebrows pointing downward towards the bridge of his nose. His nostrils expanded and his teeth gnashed. He pushed his fists towards the ceiling, growling.

I sank into a deep stance then stepped back with my palms facing him. I figured it was time to use some of my more serious techniques. I had one in mind—not one of the forbidden techniques I knew, but it'd be enough to put the giant down. He scowled at me and I scowled back. He dropped his arms in preparation to charge at me. Before he made his first stride, we were both caught by surprise, he more than me. Two loud booms stuffed the room. Okamoto continued to glare at me. His angry penetrating stare morphed into bewilderment. He lurched forward a step, dropped to his knees, then fell to his face and kissed the floor.

Standing behind him was a panting Davis with his rifle aimed where the giant once stood. Davis jogged over to me.

"You okay, Black?" he asked.

I relaxed. "I'm okay. Rose and Nicole?"

"They're fine. They're outside with Daniels."

Davis surveyed the area. He looked at the disheveled dining room, the hole in the wall, and the marred bodies lying around. "Wow! What happened here? Things didn't go quite as planned, I see."

"Nope, but the outcome was the same. We're standing. They're not," I replied.

We heard the front door slap open. I glanced around the dining room and spotted the MP5K that I had used earlier resting on the floor. I picked it up then ducked into the living room with Davis behind me. We stepped into the large foyer area. Evans' corpse was still there, Uchida's sawed-off shotgun remained positioned on the floor, but Uchida was gone. The right front door was open. I looked through it and saw Uchida hobbling across the grass into the rayless morning night. I zipped through the door and ran towards him while Davis coursed after me.

Outside, the roar of the helicopter swooped over the entire estate. The sound of police sirens rolled in from the near distance. I was maybe three or four yards away from Uchida before a voice cried out from the west side of the yard.

"D— don't move, you monster!" Nicole screamed.

Uchida paused, not because of the tone Nicole carried in her voice, but because of the gun she was pointing at him.

CHAPTER
TWENTY-ONE

It was the same Glock 22 she had borrowed from me, which I had borrowed from Rose. Uchida froze solid and gawked at Nicole, unwavering. The gun quaked in her hand from her trembling.

Rose was a few steps behind Nicole. "Hold up, wa— wait, Mrs. Burns," she called to Nicole.

"Where's my daughter and husband, you bastard?!" Nicole cried, moving closer towards Uchida.

Daniels dragged in from the west side of the yard. Davis walked up to my left side. We all observed as Uchida glanced around and cringed in fear.

"I— I— I don't know, please don't kill me," he sobbed.

A gust of wind swept through as the helicopter flew in towards the back of the house to land on the helipad. I continued to view the interaction between Nicole and Uchida in disgust.

What a coward. All the murdering and kidnapping you did, and now you want someone to show you mercy. A part of me wanted Nicole to pull the trigger, but I knew there was more at stake, and he had answers the authorities needed.

"Mrs. Burns," I called. "Your daughter and husband are both safe, as promised."

I moved closer to Nicole, who at the time had the gun inches from the head of a scared, injured, and copiously perspiring Uchida.

"Mrs. Burns, there are other concerned parents like yourself out there thinking the worst case scenario about their little girls. Although he is a sorry excuse of a human being," —I glimpsed down at Uchida—"he has information that can help other mothers find rest."

I put my hand over the top of the gun and guided it downward. As I lightly wrenched it from her hands, she broke into tears. I turned towards Uchida, who gave me a distasteful leer. I watched him with a rigid stare, hoping he would say something, so I'd have a reason to go upside his head with the pistol.

He said nothing.

Daniels came up to comfort Nicole while Davis approached to keep an eye on Uchida. The red and blue lights from the local PD were making their way to the house. I turned my attention from Uchida and walked over to Rose. She smiled at me. I smiled back.

I handed her the Glock and the MP5K. "I better get to the helicopter. I don't think I should be around for all of this. I mean, I am a civilian after all."

Rose grinned, "You're right, you are. Plus you're soaked and you look tired, you poor boy."

I chuckled. "So you're fine wrapping the rest of this up without me?"

Rose looked down then glanced up at me with another smile. "I'm sure we'll manage, Mr. Black." She then stepped around me. "Hey, Daniels, you want to do the honors?" she asked.

Daniels was embracing Nicole but looked back.

Rose raised a zip tie in the air. "Read him his rights," she said.

I looked back, smiled, and then started down the west wall of the house towards the helipad. I waited alone in the cabin of the helicopter for a little over an hour, during which I removed my Kevlar vest and comm gear. I was resting my eyes most of the time. It was quiet with the helicopter's engine switched off. The pilot was in the cockpit, probably resting his eyes as well. Everyone else was wandering about Uchida's residence, cooperating with the local law enforcement. It wasn't long before I heard footsteps rasping across the grass then scraping over the concrete of the helipad towards the helicopter. The door slid open then Rose peeped in.

"You're okay back here, Black?" she asked.

I was leaning back with my eyes half shut. I nodded.

"The medics are treating the wounded. You're not hurt, are you?"

I shook my head.

"It's a madhouse out here," Rose sighed. "Other agencies will probably be lurking around here soon. Apparently this is a big deal."

I fully opened my eyes and raised my body in the seat. "Umph... what other agencies?"

"Maybe the DHS... and I know Interpol will be involved. There'll be a lot of snooping around here. Don't worry, though, you were only here as an observer," Rose smiled.

I smiled back.

"Once Mrs. Burns and Daniels get cleared by the medics we'll be on our way." Rose ducked out and rolled the door closed.

I lounged back into thought. After another twenty-five minutes or so, we were in the air heading back to the Coast Guard base in Charleston. We left just as we had arrived except we had two additional passengers with us—Nicole and Daniels. Everyone was worn out from all that had happened over the course of the last few days. We made it to the base in just a little over an hour. The coruscant morning sun bloomed from over the Atlantic, chasing the early morning shade away.

The helicopter landed and the group of us dragged into the base. The pilot stayed behind to run some checks on the chopper. Hicks was waiting for us inside the base just outside of the command center room holding a cup of joe in his hand, which looked like it might have been his fourth cup since we last saw him.

"Welcome back," he greeted us.

The two lieutenants continued down the hall.

Rose and Davis paused to have a few words with Hicks while I escorted Nicole and Daniels to the lounge area where Burns and Madeline were resting. Father and daughter were sleeping peacefully on the couch just as they had been before we'd left. Nicole stepped into the room first, and then Daniels, and I fell in last. Nicole walked over to the couch, bent over, and tapped Burns on the shoulder. He stretched awake, released a semi-yawn, and rubbed his eyes. Once he realized it was Nicole, he jerked his body upward and a smile hit his face. Madeline was resting in his lap, so the shock woke her. He stood up and hugged his wife. Madeline joined in, and after a while Daniels did as well. There was a lot of hugging, kissing, and crying. I watched from a safe distance. Nicole looked over to me and her lips moved. She was thanking me. I nodded then quietly walked to the restroom located at the back of the room; when I returned, I just slid past them out of the room. I was happy for them, but I figured I'd give them their space—plus, it really wasn't my scene.

I walked down the hall and saw Rose and Davis exiting out of the front. I caught up with them.

"So, who's taking me to Sully Island?" I asked.

"Sully Island?" Davis inquired.

211

"What for?" Rose asked.

"I have to get my car," I said.

Both of them laughed.

We walked across the pavement and out of the gate towards the unmarked car. Davis was putting their gear in the trunk of the car.

"You're not tired?" Rose asked.

"A little, but I can manage a three, three and a half-hour drive back," I said.

The three of us hopped in the car. Davis drove, Rose was in the front passenger seat, and I sat in the back. After about thirty-five minutes of driving, we arrived at the hangar where Burns had been held. There was caution tape around the area, but we were able to work our way around it. I jumped out, strolled over to my baby, unlocked the door, sank under the steering wheel, and fired it up. I crept up to Rose and Davis and rolled down the window, signaling Davis to roll down his.

Rose leaned over Davis. "We're heading back to the base to rest, then we're going to make sure Daniels and the Burns are situated."

I saluted them then pulled off.

I drove a bit over three and a half hours, only stopping once for gas before pulling into my driveway. The late morning sun was shining marvelously and the sky, absent of clouds, gleamed a bold blue. I took it all in for a moment before circling around my yard. I marched back to the car, removed my travel bag from the trunk, and went in the house. My first stop was a shower and change of clothes; next I was in the kitchen eating fruit. Finally, I was back in my room. I darkened the windows with a blanket then plummeted to my bed. I slept until the same time the next day—about twenty-four hours.

During the following two weeks I contemplated many things. I thought about Rose and the investigation. I thought about Daniels, the Burns family, and Davis. And although money wasn't an issue for me, I pondered getting a day job. It was a brief thought because I knew me being stuck in an office or punching someone's time clock wasn't going to happen. I decided I'd do some traveling. I figured I could sell the house. The domestication thing wasn't panning out for me. I could sell most of what I had and hit the road.

I already had the "For sale" sign up and was doing a little work in the yard one day when an unmarked car pulled into my driveway. The driver side door swung open, two feet smacked the concrete of the driveway, and in front of me emerged Rose. I stood on the lawn near the front door, a smile striking my face. She was smiling as she walked towards me in her pantsuit and sunglasses.

"Good morning, Mr. Black," she said, ripping the sunglasses from her face. She was stunning.

"Morning, Special Agent Lee," I responded.

She glanced at my yard sign. "Oh... you're moving?"

"Yeah."

"Really... Where to?"

"Um... Not sure yet."

"You know, you're not in trouble. If anything, you should be getting another medal for what you've done," Rose smiled.

"It's not that... Just, things like that whole mess have a way of showing up at my doorstep. So I figured if I don't have a house, it can't show up. But regardless, I'm sure it'll be a couple of months or so before I close a sale."

"I think everyone will miss you. I mean me, Davis, and the Bureau appreciated what you've done. Daniels, I'm sure, is very grateful to you, and the Burns family has asked about you every time I've talked to them. You're a special guy, Black."

I smiled in reply.

"And there are a lot of other people who may not know you but I'm sure are thankful."

I tilted my head in confusion.

"Thanks to some information we got from Uchida, Bennett, and the bunch, we were able to uncover some hard evidence. We looked into Uchida's various investments, the flight plan of the *Carolina Dance*, some international contacts of Uchida's... and while working with Interpol we were able to make some high-profile arrests in an international human trafficking ring. There were many lost individuals found. Maybe a couple hundred—and we found four of the girls who were missing from here in the Carolinas."

I nodded, "That's good... I guess."

"Good... you guess?!" Rose responded. "It's great news."

"I'm just doing the math. Daniels and Burns were investigating four missing girls in the Carolinas and, according to you and Davis, there were seven more missing before that. That's a total of eleven. We found the two girls in Charleston, and four were found overseas, but that still leaves five missing girls," I sighed.

Rose shook her head. "Black, you can't look at it that way," she said. "There were plenty of others around the world who were found, who were rescued. You should know better than anyone that situations like these never turn out perfect."

She moved closer to me and her voice softened. "I think you wanted things to end perfectly since you were involved. Give yourself a break. Things are developing great with only three days of involvement from you."

Rose was right. I wanted everything to pan out perfectly. I wanted all of the girls to be found and all the questions to be answered right now, but I knew that's not how these types of things work. I didn't understand why I cared so much. I had kept my promise to Nicole, but I felt responsible for the others since the problem had showed up at my feet.

"You're right," I replied.

"Yeah, you and Daniels both are beating yourselves up.

Daniels still hasn't forgiven himself for giving up the where-abouts of Nicole. Although everyone else has let it go."

"About that... I never got the story behind his capture."

"Well, apparently after our meet in Rock Hill, Daniels went back to the police station to work that lead on Made-line's kidnapping. He says Williams got the drop on him."

"I told Daniels to watch out for Williams."

"They captured Daniels and took him to some hideout just outside of Gastonia. They had Madeline there too at the time and threatened to hurt her and Burns if Daniels didn't give up the location of Nicole. So he did."

I nodded. "Nicole's family?"

"They're okay. Just some property damage caused by Okamoto and the Kwon twins."

"Well, none of them should be a problem for anyone else."

Rose chuckled, "Hey, did you know Burns is being considered for the new police chief?"

"Really?"

"Yep... The previous chief, Richard Day, was found in his car near Gastonia. He was choked to death."

"Okamoto's work," I replied.

"Yep, and guess what was in the trunk of his car."

"A bag with two hundred and thirty-four thousand dollars of cash inside of it."

"Yes again... the missing money from the drug bust that Burns was rumored to have stolen when he went missing. You know, you are pretty good at this, Black. Ever thought about joining the FBI?"

I shook my head. "I've already served my time."

"I think you like it."

"Excuse me?"

"Why did you get involved with all of this?"

I smiled, "Well, someone put me in handcuffs for no reason... And then after that, I made someone a promise I had to follow through on."

"You made Nicole a promise."

"Exactly."

"Do you know why you made that promise?"

I shrugged.

"I think it's because you care. You saw a problem and you wanted to help. It's okay to want to help. That means you're a good person."

"Thank you, Freud."

We both laughed then stared into each other's eyes for a moment.

"Look, Black, I have to get back to work."

"Right."

"We all should get together. Don't be a stranger the remainder of your time here."

"I'll try not to be," I smiled.

Rose pivoted in the direction of her car then spun back towards me impulsively. She jumped in my arms and we kissed hard for a long moment.

"Just in case," she said before slowly tearing herself from my arms and strolling back to the unmarked car.

I watched with a smile on my face as she slid back into the car and reversed out of my driveway. I eased inside the house, washed up, and changed my clothes. Then I wandered into the living room. I glanced over at my coffee table and noticed the steak knife I had borrowed from the donut shop where Daniels and I had lost Evans. It had been sitting there for over two weeks. After giving it a good washing, I wrapped it inside a clean cloth and stuffed it in my coat pocket. I decided I would return the knife while it was fresh on my mind. It took me roughly fifteen or twenty minutes of driving before I reached The Donut Basement.

I sprang out of my car, entered the shop, and slid into a booth. I jabbed my hand into my pocket and carefully removed the wrapped steak knife. I unrolled it then placed the knife on top of the table. A few minutes later a waitress approached me. It was the same waitress who had served Daniels and me close to two weeks before. The beautiful, brown-skinned twenty-something-year-old with the wonderful natural hair, dressed in her waitress uniform.

"Good morning, sir," she said. "Can I start you off with something to drink?"

"No, I think I know what I want. I'll have your sausage, egg, and cheese biscuit with a black coffee, all to go please."

The waitress jotted with her pen onto her pad. "Would you like anything else?"

The moment she uttered the last syllable, something caught my eye—or rather, someone. From out of the kitchen walked a girl, one I had seen before. One of the girls I had seen at Uchida's residence in Charleston. She looked happy. She was dressed in a waitress uniform with her silky blonde hair tied in a knot. I turned my attention back to my waitress.

"I do have a question," I said. "That girl there," I threw my head in the direction of the blonde-haired girl. "How long has she been working here?"

The waitress turned to see who I was referring to.

"Oh, she just started this week. And let me tell you, she has been through some stuff recently."

"You don't say."

"Yeah, she thought she was in love. But she's cool, seems to be coping well with it. Anything else?"

I shook my head. "Nope, thank you."

A little time later the waitress came back to my table with my order in a to-go bag. I left the amount I owed plus a nice-sized tip on the table, and then slipped out of the donut shop. Outside, I looked up into a cloudless sky. The day was bright but comfortably cool. I dropped into my car, laid my bag of food in the passenger seat, and placed my coffee in the cup holder. I fired up the engine and a smile hit my face. For the first time in a while, I felt liberated.

MORE ORLANDO BLACK

YOUR NEXT EXCITING READ IS A PAGE TURN AWAY!

If you enjoyed Carolina Dance, read on for a preview of the next action-packed, thrilling Orlando Black novel by Alex Cage.

BAYSIDE BOOM

BOOK PREVIEW

CHAPTER
ONE

KEEPING IN TOUCH with family has become difficult in the modern world. Despite the technological leaps and the many avenues of long-distance contact, people are still very much disconnected from each other. Such were the thoughts Orlando Black contemplated as he sat on a bench facing the Alcatraz Shoal. The water was still and the sky was clear. The busy sound of a large crowd and many enticing aromas drifted from the various restaurants and food stands behind him. The day was sunny, quiet, and cool and Black felt comfortable in his boots, jeans, T-shirt, and light coat. He removed his cell phone from his pocket and looked at the screen before poking at it and holding it to his ear. After a few rings, a female's voice eased on the line.

"Hello?"

"How are you?" Black asked.

"Wow. Well, if it isn't the winner of this year's Worst Brother Award."

"I won again this year?"

"You seem to win every year." The voice chuckled. "Where are you?"

"Fisherman's Wharf."

"What? You're in San Francisco?"

"Yep. I thought I'd drop by and surprise my little sister."

"Aw, how sweet. Maybe you don't deserve that award after all. But I'm actually not in town."

"Oh really? Where are you?"

"I'm in Chicago right now."

"Chicago?"

"You know I've been bouncing around for work since the whole military thing. I don't think the Corps would take me back."

"Well, you did break your C.O.'s jaw."

"That sexist pig had it coming. It can be so hard for women in the Marines."

"So what are you doing in Chicago?"

"I have a private security gig I'm working."

"Be careful with those companies."

"Oh, now you want to put on your big bro pants and protect me?"

"I'm serious."

"Chill out."

"Olivia Jane Black, I mean it!"

"Okay, okay, I'll be careful, and you know I don't like it when you use my full name like that."

"That's all I'm asking. There's no need to put yourself in harm's way, especially when you don't need the money."

"I can take care of myself."

Black nodded. "Yep, I know."

"Hey, have you been to see Mom and Dad?"

"No, not yet."

"Make sure you visit them."

"We'll see," he shrugged.

Olivia sighed. "Look, I know they're not blood, but I feel they're my mom and dad. Go see them, okay?"

"We'll see," Black repeated.

Multiple voices on the other end of the line filled his ear.

"I have to go," Olivia said. "I have a meeting. Love you, bye."

"Hey, be careful," Black said, but the call ended before he could finish speaking. "You too, little sis," he muttered to himself.

He sat on the bench for a while and enjoyed the view. After some time, the food smells made his stomach growl. *I better get something to eat*, he thought, patting his stomach.

He stood up from the bench and walked across the wooden pier and up a sidewalk, where he joined throngs of pedestrians. The streets were filled with food carts, balloon artists, musicians, and painters. Just about all types of performance entertainment were present. Black fought through the crowd and crossed the street, where he ran into an entirely different group of people. They were marching around the deck of Pier 39, thrusting large signs into the air. He read a few of the signs. One read, *I can have as many kids as I want*. Another, *In memory of the brave in New York*, and yet another, *Say NO to P.L. 324!* He stopped walking, curious. A young lady from the group approached him.

With her fingertips, she brushed her fine blond hair behind her ear and smiled. "Hi, sir, are you here to march with us?"

"What?"

The young lady extended a flier. "We're here to stop the public law 324 that the president is trying to pass."

Black looked down at the flier. In large font stood the number 324 with a circle around it and a line crossing through it. Below the circle was written, *Kids are precious*, and under that there was a description that compared a president he hadn't voted for nor cared about to a donkey. There was also today's date, a time frame, and the location of Fisherman's Wharf. Black looked at the girl and was about to speak, but a guy who looked to be in his early twenties stepped up and put his arms around the young lady, kissing her on the cheek.

"What's up, babe, who's this?" he asked.

"This is a gentleman who I believe wants to march with us," she said, smiling and raising her eyebrows.

"Oh, so you're here for the protest?"

Black shook his head. "I don't even know what you're protesting."

"324," the guy said.

Black stared at him.

"Basically the government is saying if we have more than five children we have to pay a population tax. Crazy, right?"

"We should be able to have as many kids as we want," the young lady added.

"So are you guys planning on having six kids?" Black asked.

"No," they said in sync.

"Do you have any kids?"

"No," they said again.

Black said nothing.

"But we have rights," the girl said.

"Yeah, it's just wrong, dude. And we're not going to let what the government did in New York scare us," the guy said.

Black squinted as the couple was pulled away by the crowd, marching down the street and chanting in protest.

He shrugged and walked off across the pier. As he entered a restaurant, he noticed a camera above the door. Inside were many empty tables, a couple of waiters, and a bartender. The ceiling fan squeaked and the smell of seafood and alcohol stuffed the place. Black creaked across the wooden floor towards the bar. He sat on a stool and lifted a menu from the counter. The bartender was cleaning a glass. He wore a white button-down shirt with the sleeves rolled up to his forearms. There was a black apron across his waist above his black slacks. He finished washing the glass and draped the cloth he used to dry it over his shoulder before looking over at Black.

"So, what can I start you off with?" he asked.

"I'll start with a water," Black said.

"You got it." The bartender grabbed a glass, filled it with water, and slid it in front of Black. "It's a madhouse out there, huh?"

Black began looking through the menu. "The West Coast is usually a madhouse when it comes to political issues," he said.

"Well, the East Coast has been chaotic as of late too," the bartender said, craning over and wiping the countertop.

Black looked at him.

The bartender stood straight, looking at Black. "Oh, you haven't been watching the news?" he asked.

"I've been on the road a lot."

The bartender grabbed the remote and turned on the TV, which hung suspended over the bar.

Black looked as the screen flicked on, displaying some news broadcast. A pretty news anchor was speaking. Imposed next to her face was a rectangular box showing footage of New York City, near Times Square. There was a lot of smoke and people. Emergency responders were every-where. Black's sharp eyes quickly picked out *324* and *bombing* in the headline at the bottom of the screen.

"It's still unclear how the peaceful protest of two days ago turned into a chaotic and gruesome scene," the reporter said.

Black sighed and shook his head before turning his attention back to the menu.

"Pretty unfortunate," the bartender said.

"Yes, it is."

"Some believe the government had something to do with it."

"So I heard."

"What do you make of it?"

Black looked at the bartender. "Make of what? The bombing or the law?"

"Well, both I guess."

"I don't know, but I don't think the government is behind the bombing."

"What makes you say that?"

"If government officials want something to happen, they create laws, which is what they're doing in this case. It's business to them. Whoever is behind the bombing feels a personal attachment to what they believe the law stands for. This person feels victimized. They probably feel that if the law were in place they would've never been a victim."

The bartender nodded.

"As for the law itself, I don't think I care either way. I don't have any kids nor do I plan on having any."

"Personally I'm for it. I don't care what all these rights activists are saying. If you're collecting a check from the government and you have more than three kids, you should get snipped."

"Snipped?"

"Man, you really haven't been watching the news. If you get government assistance and you have more than three kids, 324 says you have to get snipped or tied to continue receiving assistance."

"I heard it was five kids."

"That's for everyone, assistance or not. If you have more than five kids you have to pay some type of tax."

Black quietly looked at the menu.

The bartender began washing glasses. "It makes sense to me," he said. "I believe it'll help with many of the issues we face in this country. I was reading somewhere that something like ninety percent of criminals come from a fatherless home."

The bartender continued talking while Black stared up at the TV, watching scenes from the tragic event.

. . .

FORTY MINUTES LATER Black was back outside. The group of protesters had nearly doubled in size. He shook his head. *What do they believe they're going to accomplish?* He began to thread through the noisy crowd. Then something caught his eye. One of the protesters, a slender guy, was wearing a dark coat, cap, and shades. In one of his hands was a sign that read, *NO 324!* and in his other a small duffel bag. He eased his way through the people, blending in. He stopped and carefully looked around before gently dropping the duffel bag to the wooden deck of the pier. He then walked away quickly. Black walked after the guy, but then he heard his commanding officer's voice from back in his military days: *If they drop it to the ground, chances are it can make a kaboom sound.* He looked at the duffel bag and spotted some wiring through the zipper slit. Squatting, he unzipped the bag. His eyes slightly widened, his mouth gaped open, and he felt drops of sweat blooming around his neck. Inside the bag was a home-made bomb. Small, but big enough to cause some damage.

Black snatched the bag, pushing and shoving through the crowd. "Out of the way! Move! Get out of the way!" He ran to the edge of the pier and lobbed the bag over the waves with all his might. His body draped over the railing as he watched the bag sink into the water. As it dropped just below the surface there was an ear-rocking boom.

THANK YOU FOR READING

I have a favor to ask. If you have a moment, I would really appreciate it if you could leave a short review on the page where you purchased this book. I'm thankful for you sharing your feedback about this book. It really helps new readers find this series.

Sign up for notifications of new books by Alex Cage and exclusive giveaways

www.AlexCage.com/signup

ALSO BY ALEX CAGE

More books by Alex Cage. Have you read them all? Grab your next adventure today!

Orlando Black Series

Carolina Dance

Bayside Boom

Family Famous (Novella)

Bet on Black

Leroy Silver Series

Contracts & Bullets

Aloha & Bullets

Get the latest releases and exclusive giveaways, sign up to the Alex Cage Reader List.

www.AlexCage.com/signup

JOIN THE READER'S LIST

Get the latest releases and exclusive giveaways - sign up to the Alex Cage Reader List:

www.AlexCage.com/signup

ABOUT THE AUTHOR

Alex Cage is a thriller author and passionate wordsmith who loves to blend his fascination with martial arts and travel with high-octane action and explosive adventures. He enjoys nothing more than entertaining his readers with death-defying missions, larger-than-life characters, and suspenseful stories that always find a way to keep you on your toes.

As the author of nearly a dozen titles, including the Orlando Black series and the Leroy Silver series, Alex combines his obsession for thrillers with a sprinkling of fantasy and sci-fi, so that readers will always find something to capture their imagination. He currently resides in North Carolina. When not writing his next novel, you can find him reading and practicing martial arts.

Find out more about Alex Cage (and get a free read):

www.alexcage.com
connect@alexcage.com

CLEAN FAST-PACED ACTION THRILLERS

Made in United States
Orlando, FL
22 June 2023

34430160R00157